AMONG THE LOST

Among the Lost

Robert Davis

Lost Books Press
San Francisco, California

OTHER BOOKS BY ROBERT DAVIS:

Kimura (Walker and Company, 1989)
Iz (Lost Books Press, 1995)

AMONG THE LOST
©November 2009

Published in the United States by Lost Books Press.

Library of Congress Control Number: 2009910939

All rights reserved. No part of this publication may be reproduced, stored in a retrieval system, or transmitted, in any form or by any means, electronic, mechanical, photocopying, recording, or otherwise, without the written prior permission of the author.

Text copyright ©2009 by Robert Davis
Design by Winslow Colwell/WColwell Design

Cover photographs used with grateful permission of members of the Cuban-American exchange, September 1964.

The text of this publication was set in Adobe Minion.

Printed in the United States
ISBN 978-0-9645592-1-9

For further information, or to reproduce selections from this book, write:
Lost Books Press
PO Box 31438
San Francisco, CA 94131

www.lostbookspress.com

For Carole

Many shades of the departed are occupied solely in licking at the waves of the river of death because it flows from our direction and still has the salty taste of our seas. Then the river rears back in disgust, the current flows the opposite way and brings the dead drifting back into life.

— Kafka

1

In 1964 Felicia Vasquez was the West Coast organizer for the Fair Play for Cuba Committee, a group which had become notorious after Lee Harvey Oswald's alleged membership in it. Writing about this group for my newspaper, the *Free Express*, I met and fell in love with Felicia. She was a beautiful woman with olive skin, fine black hair, deep brown eyes, and an extraordinary passion. Unlike other true believers I met in Berkeley during the Sixties, she'd studied history and economics, and could argue intelligently for her cause.

The first time I heard Felicia speak was on the university campus. I couldn't decide whether to remain at the back of the lecture hall, where I had a good view of her, or to move to the front row and get as close as possible. I was thinking she must have Indian blood because she looked almost oriental. Her clothes—bright oranges, reds and greens—reminded me of flamenco dancers and gypsies I'd seen in movies. During the question period I asked why anyone should risk jail by joining the trip to Cuba she was organizing. Wouldn't Communists lead American students around by the nose? Wasn't such a trip just propaganda? Felicia answered all my questions. However, when I got back to the office, I realized I hadn't written anything down. Still, her main point was clear—people should see for themselves and make up their own minds.

A week later, covering another political meeting, I was bored, and to stay awake I was playing mental chess, taking both sides, until somebody in the room started shouting and I lost track of the game and went to my fall-back position—practicing self-hypnosis, trying to make my left arm levitate without consciously using any muscles. This was a question of mind over matter. I became so absorbed that I didn't notice Felicia's entrance. Then, just as I was succeeding and my arm was going up in the air, there was a vote. I was pleased. I was smiling. I didn't realize I'd just voted against an important motion until this passionate woman accosted me. When I figured out what she was talking about, I tried to explain about self-hypnosis and mind over matter. Felicia Vasquez stared at me as if I were a lunatic. For a moment I thought she was going to hit me. Instead, she burst out laughing. That did it. I was in love. The next time I saw her, I asked for a date.

I was so young then—full of myself, full of vague ambitions and longings. No career appealed to me. I wanted significance; I wanted meaning in my life.

With the post-World War II prosperity, my family had left the tenements of San Francisco's Mission District and moved to the west side, the Sunset District, a neighborhood of tract houses built over sand dunes, the sand dunes infested with fleas and covered by fog or gray clouds, a grid of plaster and cement where sheep-like men filed onto streetcars in the morning and returned as whipped dogs in the evening. Growing up as an Italian in a sea of Irish, I was an outsider. The camera my grandfather gave me was my one true friend. I preferred to read or, better yet, to go to the movies. The Parkside Theater was my church.

I graduated from college in 1963, the year Kennedy was shot, Martin Luther King said, "I have a dream," the Beatles recorded "I Want to Hold Your Hand," the first artificial heart was installed, and Valium came on the market. My roommate and best friend was Charley Jessup, who studied art while I studied philosophy, which meant that neither of us knew much about the real world. For example, to me Cuba meant bearded adventurers who drank rum with Ernest Hemingway and in 1962 had recklessly brought the world to the brink of nuclear war. But Charley and I, on our late night walks, preferred to argue about Dostoevsky or Kant, Russell or Wittgenstein.

One afternoon in my first semester of graduate school, distracted by notes in the margins of a book I should have been studying, I wondered why this marginalia was more interesting to me than the text itself. Staring vacantly across the library, I suddenly saw myself as an old man, sitting in this same chair, but the marginal notes would be my own—the story of a pathetic life. I felt as if I were drowning. That afternoon I telephoned Charley in New York, where he was checking out art schools, and told him I was quitting school. The next week I moved into an apartment in my grandfather's building in the Haight-Ashbury, and I soon became friends—or at least acquaintances—with the hippies and old beatniks who hung out in the coffee houses on Haight Street.

My first job was as a social worker. The most important part of the job was to make sure the clients didn't get too much money. I lasted three months. My next job was as a loan officer trainee. The boss was a man named Snow, who signed his name with two vertical lines through the 'S.' When I approved my first loan application, Mr. Snow couldn't believe I wanted to give money to people with no assets. Even worse, I hadn't checked the form to indicate the applicants were black.

According to my father, I was supposed to be thankful for this job, thankful for the opportunity to be exploited, thankful that at the end of the week I got a paycheck which allowed me to survive for another period of debasement. I was not thankful. I hated Mr. Snow. I hated application forms that had to be checked in the proper place if the applicant was black. I sent some photographs I'd taken of a civil rights demonstration, along with a brief article about the demonstration, to the *Free Express*, a new Berkeley newspaper. The editor and publisher, Mary Wilson, a middle-aged former socialite who now wore overalls and smoked a pipe, asked me to come in. At the interview I said I was passionate about photography and was willing to dig for the truth. I also admitted, proudly, that I'd probably wind up in some gutter as my father predicted, but I didn't care.

Mrs. Wilson hired me on the spot.

Felicia Vasquez lived in San Francisco's Latin neighborhood, the Mission. The first thing I noticed at her apartment was that the walls were covered with pictures of Cuban leaders. On our first date we went to an old movie, *The Treasure of the Sierra Madre*, and afterwards, walking along the waterfront, came upon a scene which itself could have been part of that movie. One of the newspapers was running a contest, a treasure hunt, and each day published clues about where Emperor Norton had buried his gold. This particular evening the beach at Aquatic Park was covered with people digging holes. Felicia and I looked on as they tore up the beach, while in the harbor sailboats rocked peacefully at anchor. Back at her apartment we listened to Bob Dylan. Her dog, a German shepherd, lay at our feet as we talked about revolution. Didn't "revolution," I said, mean returning to the place where you began?

She stared at me. I needed to educate myself, she said, not simply accept the propaganda I'd been hearing all my life. What did I really know about the Russian Revolution before Stalin came to power? What did I know about the Cuban Revolution?

Sometime after midnight she was sitting next to me on the sofa, showing me photos she'd taken in Cuba during the Literacy Campaign, when she fell asleep. She was so close that if I moved I'd wake her. I sat still until she woke on her own. When I left, it was with an armful of books. I took them partly as an excuse to come back.

As I dug through these books, I began to see that the history I'd been taught in school was not the whole truth. Reading about Trotsky's escape from Siberia in a troika, I felt as if I were in a troika myself, crossing new frontiers, a vast extension of the principles of the Enlightenment, principles I agreed with. Or was I merely heading into the wastelands of another Siberia?

In spite of our different backgrounds, we became lovers. In early spring we went to Big Sur. We stood for hours on a hillside and looked at the stars and the ocean, and talked. We hiked through forests and followed a stream to the top of a mountain, where I took her photograph. We walked into a silent canyon, and, looking up at the roots of trees clinging to the edges of the cliffs, Felicia said, "Sometimes trees grow in strange places."

"Sometimes trees grow in strange places." These words have stayed with me.

I decided that if her Cuba trip took place, I wanted to be on it. But the project was at risk for several reasons. Most importantly the government was harassing the Fair Play for Cuba Committee. I decided to write an article about this harassment. I was enthusiastic, perhaps because I was in love. When we got back from Big Sur, I came to the Fair Play office to work on a story. Felicia and I were at her desk in the second floor office when three men entered, pointed guns at us, and, shouting in Spanish, told us to lie on the floor. Because none of the men wore a mask, I thought they were going to kill us. As I hesitated to get onto the floor, one of them pushed me. I turned to fight, but Felicia pulled me back. A woman named Monica Chapman came in with a cup of coffee, and was also told to lie on the floor. She swore at the men, didn't get onto the floor fast enough. They pushed her. Then the men, who spoke with what Felicia said was definitely a Cuban accent, splashed gasoline around the office. They told us to stay where we were, set the place on fire, and ran down the stairs.

At least they hadn't shot us. We all got out, and the fire was extinguished before it caused much damage. At the police station we were shown photographs. Felicia told the police she'd seen one of the men previously and that he worked for an organization called Cuba Libre, which had an office in San Francisco. The police noted this down. Felicia asked them to show us their files of Cuban exile groups, but the sergeant said such files didn't exist.

"And if they did, you would have to talk to the FBI," he added, giving us the impression that the police were not only uninterested in Cuban exiles, but that they might even be protecting them. This, I thought, might make an interesting story. So, without telling my boss what I was doing, I decided to see what I could uncover about Cuban exiles.

The group called Cuba Libre had an office on Fremont Street in San Francisco. The day after the fire I went there. A directory said Cuba Libre was on the fourth floor. I went up. Two men were sitting behind desks. I recognized one of them as one of the arsonists. Hastily I said I had the wrong office, left, and went across the street and to a coffee shop where I could watch the entrance of the building. At noon the two men came out. I followed them down Fremont Street. They went into a restaurant. I kept walking, then turned around, and from a doorway across the street I waited some more. After half an hour they emerged and went back to their office building, and I went back to the coffee shop. Before I could call Felicia or the police, one of the men—the man I'd recognized as one of the arsonists and whom I now dubbed 'Cantinflas' because he resembled the Mexican actor—came out of the building. Again I followed. He went to the parking lot where my own car was parked, pulled out, and headed south. He drove to 24th and Harrison, parked, and went into a café.

From the street I could see inside the café, and saw that Cantinflas was sitting with another man. I parked up the street. Finally the other man, a Latino with a mustache and goatee, came out and walked past me. Then Cantinflas came out and drove away, this time to the Western Addition where he entered an apartment building.

At home I called Felicia and then the police, and told them where to find one of the arsonists. I gave the police both the address on Fremont Street and the address in the Western Addition. The next day I was told there was no such office on Fremont Street. And, indeed, when I returned, the Cuba Libre office was vacant. Cantinflas didn't show up again at the apartment house I'd seen him enter.

I wrote up what I knew about the attack on Fair Play, and how the Cuba Libre organization had disappeared immediately after I'd notified the police. By this time the newspaper treasure hunt Felicia and I had witnessed at Aquatic Park had taken over the city, and people were everywhere digging up gardens and parks. The contest was even called "The Treasure of the Sierra Madre." So in my article I wrote that in San Francisco the "Federales" did not chase or arrest bandits but were in cahoots with them, and that depending on our police to find these arsonists was as futile as trying to find the gold dust which, in the movie, was blown across the desert.

I thought this was clever writing. But shortly after my article appeared Felicia told me she was being followed.

"This may have been going on for a long time," she said. "I've had this feeling before."

"Gusanos?" This is what Felicia called the Cubans who had set fire to her office.

"I don't know."

By the end of April the Cuba trip, co-sponsored by the Federation of Cuban University Students, had gotten quite a bit of publicity, and a group called the People's Revolutionary Party wanted to talk to Felicia about combining her trip with one they were planning.

"I don't think much will come of it," Felicia told me. She referred to them as "ultra-lefts," "Third Period Stalinists," and a few other political labels I was unfamiliar with. "But I'm going to talk to them," she said. "Do you want to come?"

I was anxious to cover an event sponsored by the Sexual Freedom League, so we made a date for the next day.

I still regret not going with Felicia that night.

2

When I got home, I called Felicia, but she wasn't back yet. In the morning I tried her at the Fair Play office, but she hadn't come in yet. I decided to surprise her and take her to breakfast. My place was a fifteen-minute drive from Felicia's apartment on Precita Avenue.

Her building faced a park of scrubby grass which separated the two sides of Precita. She liked to let her dog run there, but mostly she'd walk him up the Bernal Hill where there was a good view of the bay—although if the wind was wrong, the smell of the Butcher Town slaughterhouses could be overwhelming. Felicia's apartment was on the top floor. An outside stairway divided the building, three apartments on one side, three on the other. I parked in front, climbed the stairs, and knocked. There was no answer. I knocked again. Had I missed her? Was she already on her way to her office? I was about to leave when I heard Camillo whining inside. I called out. Maybe Felicia was in the back and hadn't heard me. I tried the door. It was unlocked. She must have been expecting me. I opened the door and called again. A nasty odor confronted me in the hallway. Camillo, sitting with his ears pointed up, turned to me and howled.

"Felicia?"

I entered. Remembering it now, I seemed to move through the tunnel-like entrance of her hallway in slow motion, as if carried, exerting no effort of my own, like Alice falling down the rabbit hole.

The apartment consisted of the long hallway with rooms to the left. On the right, a wall separated the apartments. The front room, its windows facing the street, was her study. It contained a desk and book cases crammed with books. Next was the bathroom, its door closed. I stopped, called, and moved on to the bedroom. The bedroom door was open. The bed was unmade but empty. At the far end of the hall was the kitchen, clean but empty, then a porch and a stairway leading to the yard.

I came back and knocked on the bathroom door. Camillo stared up at me. When he pushed his paw against the door, I turned the handle.

Felicia lay naked in her bathtub, partly under water. Her eyes were open. The bath water was discolored. The room stank. Staring down at her, I felt like I was drowning myself. When I imagine the scene now, it's as if she's lost in thought, the ends of her black hair floating over her shoulders.

She'd been dead for hours. That's what the cops said. The detectives said it looked like suicide, probably from a drug overdose.

"Is she Mexican?" the fat cop, Detective Mantz, said. He said this in a tone of voice which implied that drugs and suicide were what one should expect from Mexicans.

I said I was her friend and that I'd come to take her to breakfast. I said that when I'd heard the dog whining, I'd tried the door and entered.

Watching the police move around the apartment, I thought absurd things like, Felicia could've done x or y, but she'd done z, and so she'd died, but z made no difference because it equalled x, and x equalled y, and suicide made no sense, and life is full of paradoxes and ambiguities and contradictions. Perhaps my old roommate, Charley Jessup, was right. He liked to say everything could be reduced to the "nothingness" it would become in the long run.

There was something wrong about the way Felicia lay in the tub. It was a large old bathtub with claw feet. Maybe it was because her muscles had gone slack. But there was something else. While the police moved around the apartment, I went to the back porch and sat on the stairs. Just a little while ago we'd hiked in Big Sur and walked on the beaches and told each other about our childhoods. I went to the bathroom again. Then I went into the bedroom. There had been a photograph I'd taken of her at Big Sur and which she'd tacked to the wall. It was gone. I wondered when she'd taken it down. I went back to the bathroom. I don't know how long I stared, but the way her head rested was wrong. I wanted to turn her. I wanted to make her comfortable. I think I would have, but I felt the dog touching my hand. Followed by the dog, I went into the front room and stood by Felicia's desk and looked at the shelves of books as if I might find some reason there for what had happened.

"She was organizing a trip to Cuba," I told the policemen. "A student trip. The Cubans liked her idea. She'd made an arrangement with the Federation of Cuban University Students." The skinny cop was listening to me. The other one wasn't. "She was the West Coast organizer for the Fair Play for Cuba Committee," I said. "She was harassed by the FBI. Also the Fair Play Committee office was recently torched by Cuban exiles. Felicia thought she was being followed. She thought her apartment might have been searched when she wasn't home."

The fat cop now looked at me. "Are you talking about the group Lee Harvey Oswald was part of?" I wondered if he was daring me to say something un-American. Probably Felicia would have said the stuff about Oswald and Cuba was just propaganda, but what was the use? The other cop, Stringfield, said, "Who said anything about killed?"

I said, "Her head's on crooked."

Both policemen went into the bathroom. When they came back, the fat one said, "How close were you to her?"

"Pretty close."

A few minutes later the skinny cop told me to leave. He said the police would contact me later.

I gathered up Camillo's leash, bowls, and the pallet he slept on, and took him with me. He whined as I took him down the stairs. I told him he was going to live with me now. In the car he rested his head against my shoulder, and we drove to my apartment. Since my grandfather owned the building, there wouldn't be any problem. When I was a kid I'd been in a car accident—a friend had died. Other than that, the only real deaths I'd seen had been older relatives in mortuaries. Both my parents and three of my grandparents were still alive. The vision of Felicia Vasquez in the bathtub bothered me. So did the fact that the bathtub had been full of dirty water. If her neck was broken, had she been paralyzed? If she'd been paralyzed, had she been conscious as she drowned? Had she lain there unable to move, watching the tub fill with water? Thinking about this, I could hardly drive. At first I'd seen her as exotic, but then I'd gotten to know the real person, and I'd fallen in love. And now…

It was this first night that I began dreaming about her. In my dream she usually wore skirts and blouses of bright blues and yellows, reds and greens. The sun highlighted her smooth skin and black hair.

I went back to the office building on Fremont Street and to the apartment building in the Western Addition, but there was no sign of Cuba Libre. I visited the storefront office of the People's Revolutionary Party and talked to a man named Steve who told me Felicia hadn't shown up for the meeting with his people. Then I drove to Los Angeles for the funeral.

I sat in the last pew of the chapel. It was hot, and the mass dragged on and on. When it was over, a woman approached me.

"I'm Mirta, Felicia's sister," she said.

"Dante Aucielo," I said.

Mirta Vasquez was taller than her sister, and was not quite the beauty Felicia had been. She said Felicia had sent a photograph of us together, and thanked me for coming all the way from San Francisco. A Rosary had been held the day before, she said. I hadn't planned on going to the cemetery, but now it was impossible not to.

The younger children didn't show up at the cemetery. The immediate family stood around the grave site. A few yards behind the crowd sat the machine which had dug up the earth. In spite of being a small woman, Felicia's mother was an imposing figure. Looking at her, I could see where Felicia's beauty had come from, and I could imagine what Felicia might have looked like in twenty or thirty years. Then, as the coffin was lowered, the mother crumpled. Two men caught her before she fell into the grave herself. Cries, terrible, inconsolable wailing sounds, pierced the air. Until this moment I had contained myself, but now I, along with everyone else, was overwhelmed.

The Vasquez family lived on a quiet, tree-lined street in East Los Angeles. Their house was a white one-story affair, detached on both sides and indistinguishable from the other houses on the block. Rooms had been added in back. When I arrived, food and drinks were being served. The children who had been at the church were in the house and in the front and back yards. I felt out of place. But before I could escape, Mirta introduced me to her parents.

"Who would do this thing?" Mrs. Vasquez said. She looked at me from the couch in the front room where she sat surrounded by other women.

I had no answer. In the presence of a mother who had lost her child, I could only murmur condolences.

In the kitchen I talked to Felicia's brothers. In a bedroom at the back of the house, with a cup of coffee, I recounted for Mirta how I'd found Felicia's body. As I talked, Mirta Vasquez shivered.

"Were you in love with her?" she said.

Instead of answering the question, I made a stupid comment about the size of her family.

"Mostly they're friends and neighbors," Mirta said. "Everybody loved Felicia."

The Vasquez family, I learned, had come to Los Angeles from Fresno, where their father had owned land. Mr. Vasquez owned his own business. Mrs. Vasquez spoke English, but only when she had to. There were still many relatives in Mexico. The family had been divided over the Bay of Pigs invasion. In spite of political quarrels—the parents and brothers loved Kennedy, but Felicia thought Kennedy had bought the White House—Mirta said that the family was close. Felicia would telephone, write long letters, and visit regularly.

As Mirta talked, I remembered that Felicia had once asked me what it was like for me growing up. My neighborhood was all white people, I'd said, people who had absorbed the country's prejudices, who automatically hated anyone different, like beatniks—or Mexicans and blacks—and who sang patriotic songs when they were drunk.

"Jacob didn't even send a card," Mirta said.

"What?"

"Jacob Campbell."

This was the first I knew that there had been a personal association between Felicia and a man she'd vaguely mentioned.

"They were very friendly, at one time," Mirta said. "Then they weren't. The police asked about him. And about you. They said you think Cuban exiles did this."

Mirta left the room and came back with a folder which she placed on the bed. The folder contained letters, some with campus newspaper articles attached, articles which described speeches Felicia had given at different colleges as she'd gone about organizing her trip to Cuba. Some of the letters warned Felicia's parents what their daughter was doing. Others were threats sent to Felicia. All the postmarks were in the last few months.

Mirta said, "When we talked on the phone a couple of weeks ago, Felicia said she was being followed. She thought it was the FBI or Cuban exiles. She also told me that she had a serious argument with Jacob Campbell."

"About?"

Mirta shrugged. "Politics. He wanted the franchise on Cuba."

I didn't understand.

"Maybe 'franchise' isn't the right word. It's a strange organization, Dante. It started out as RPM—the Revolutionary People's Movement— then became the People's Revolutionary Party, PRP. Anyway, Campbell wanted his group to be the official Cuba support group in this country, and he thought Felicia's trip cut across this."

"Is that something people kill over?"

Mirta shrugged.

"You've met Jacob Campbell?" I asked.

"Yes."

"Do you think he could—"

"I don't like him, and I don't trust him, and I don't trust the police. I think to them my sister was just a Mexican, and Mexicans don't count. I talked to those detectives when I went to get my sister's things. I told them about these letters, but they weren't interested. I don't think they'll try very hard to find her killer."

I told Mirta about the arson attack at the Fair Play for Cuba office, and how the Cuba Libre organization had suddenly disappeared. I also said that Felicia was supposed to meet with somebody from the People's Revolutionary Party the night before she was killed, but that apparently the meeting hadn't happened. Then I asked Mirta to tell me more about Jake Campbell.

"Felicia had a bad experience with him and his group. That's what I know. She had a short affair with Campbell. But her pain was deeper because of disillusionment."

"I don't understand."

"Felicia was as passionate in condemning the mass murders of Stalin as she was passionate about condemning the crimes of capitalism in the Third World or fascism in Europe. Although she rejected the idea that all socialists, once in power, were as evil as anyone else, she saw things about this group, things we never had a chance to talk about, that led her to believe Campbell was a bad man."

On the drive back to San Francisco, I took the Coast Highway, the long route which would take me through Big Sur and which gave me time to think. I wondered again how, after all the millions who had been betrayed by Stalin, Felicia could ever have joined a group like the People's Revolutionary Party. I now considered myself a radical, of some sort, but I was repelled by groups which called themselves "Communist." I wondered if the fellow I'd talked to had lied, and if Felicia had actually met with the People's Revolutionary Party the night she was killed. I would have to dig deeper.

Drinking coffee at the same restaurant in Big Sur where Felicia and I had eaten just weeks earlier, I thought about climbing through the canyon to the top of the hills where I'd taken her picture. But I didn't. Now I wanted to get back to the city and find her killers. As I continued the drive, I kept seeing that bathtub. When I was a kid, I used to fish on the bay, and I'd had some scary experiences. Then, as a teenager, trying to impress some kids by jumping into a river from a tree, I'd almost drowned. But the worst thing had happened in a place known as Middleground, where the Sacramento and San Joaquin Rivers flow into San Francisco Bay. I'd once been stranded on a mud flat there and had almost drowned.

When I got back to the city, my father called. The police had talked to him. What was I involved in? Why was I working for a hippie newspaper and writing communist propaganda? When I tried to explain, my father raised his voice. "Where there's smoke, there's fire!" he said. When I put down the telephone, I realized that I didn't just dislike this man, whose sole ambition in life was to make money. I usually thought of him as comic, loud, a man who enjoyed public farts. But actually he was a violent man who had once pushed my mother down a flight of stairs, a man who used to punch and slap my brother and me. He would've hated Felicia Vasquez before even meeting her, because she was Mexican. He would've hated her more afterwards, because she identified with and fought for the poor. I didn't just dislike my father. I despised him.

That night I dreamed Felicia and I were caught in a storm. Our boat swamped. The motor was lost. Stunned by the sudden gale, we stood in the boat, waist-deep in water, the only sound the howling of the wind. When I woke up, I was drenched in sweat.

3

Before I had a chance to learn more about the People's Revolutionary Party, I was visited by the police, Detectives Mantz and Stringfield, and an FBI agent named Larson. Detective Mantz, who reminded me of Orson Wells in *Touch of Evil*, squeezed into my old leather chair. Larson, an older man with short gray hair, wore a blue suit and sat as if he were trying to avoid the germs on my couch. I put Camillo in the kitchen and brought in chairs for Stringfield and myself.

The FBI guy began, asking first what I knew about Felicia's involvement with "subversive" politics. I said that she was organizing a trip to Cuba, and did things like pass out leaflets and march for civil rights.

"Do you know if she had any enemies?"

"Right-wing anti-Castroites, for sure. They torched her office."

"Communist enemies?"

"She argued with lots of people about politics. I once saw her and Kenneth Rexroth go at it."

"What about?"

"Democracy. Rexroth said the Cubans were imposing totalitarianism."

"Is this Rexroth a student?"

"He's a poet and a critic. He has a program on KPFA." Although I'd agreed more with Rexroth's positions at the time, I'd been impressed by Felicia, who had held her own with the writer.

"Is he a Communist?"

"More of an anarchist, I think, and a Catholic."

"And you, Mr. Freeman? Are you a Communist?"

"I'm a Goldwater Republican."

Agent Larson stared at me. Finally he said, "Miss Vasquez didn't commit suicide. She was murdered."

I asked how he knew.

"The coroner said her neck was snapped before she was placed in the bathtub. The actual cause of death, however, was drowning."

"Would she have been conscious in the tub?"

Larson shrugged. He didn't know, but said that the landlord, Mr. Broussard, believed that between two and two thirty of the morning in question someone who was not one of his tenants had come down the outside staircase.

"He knows his tenants," Larson continued. "He's sure it was someone who doesn't live in his building. He thinks maybe it was a drug dealer. The footsteps stopped on the third step from the bottom. Mr. Broussard's bedroom is just a few feet away from the stairs at this point. He says the person paused for a minute, then jumped over the other stairs to the street."

"What's that mean?"

Larson shrugged.

"Mr. Broussard says that his own tenants never do that." "He says he's seen you do that." This was Detective Mantz.

I said that was something I would never do, at least not since I'd broken my ankle a few years ago. I turned to Stringfield. "Was she assaulted sexually?"

"The coroner couldn't tell," Larson said. "She'd been in that tub a long time."

"The obvious suspects are the Cuban exiles," I said. "These people tried to burn down the offices of the Fair Play for Cuba Committee. They threatened her. Felicia was organizing a trip to Cuba."

"You're referring to the letters her sister has," Detective Stringfield said.

"There's also a group called the People's Revolutionary Party," I said. "Felicia was supposed to have a meeting with them the night she was killed. She'd had arguments with their leader, a man named Jacob Campbell."

Detective Mantz said, "This murder might have nothing to do with politics. It could have been a lovers' quarrel."

"There was no quarrel between us."

"Miss Vasquez never showed up for that meeting with the PRP," Stringfield said. "We've already talked to them." The FBI agent then asked if I'd been planning to join Felicia's trip to Cuba. I said I'd written about

it for my newspaper, and, yes, I was considering going to Cuba.
"Did you know that she had meetings in Cuba with Che Guevara?"
"She admired the Cubans."
"Che Guevara's specialty is international subversion."
I laughed. "Felicia was only organizing a visit. I don't think you can call that subversion."
"You've been arrested for drugs," Mantz said.
"That was my former roommate."

Mantz nodded and let his partner, Stringfield, continue the questioning. They were treating me as a suspect and not a witness or as Felicia's friend. As I fended off questions and insinuations, I wondered why Larson was here. Did the FBI think Felicia was involved in some kind of guerrilla adventure? What was he not telling me? Was it true that she hadn't met with the PRP, or was this just what they'd told both me and the police? Maybe they'd come to her house. If there had been an argument and she'd gotten hurt, they'd surely try to cover it up. I supposed that as far as the cops were concerned, I worked for a subversive little Berkeley newspaper and looked like a hippie, and therefore I was "suspect." Still, why was the FBI involved? It had to be because of the Cuban exiles or the People's Revolutionary Party. I wondered if the police would pursue only lines of investigation approved by this Agent Larson.

Fair Play for Cuba held a memorial meeting for Felicia at the Unitarian Church on Franklin Street in San Francisco. The former president of the student body of the University of California, Bill Johnson, gave a speech. Bill, or BJ as he was known, was an all-American type, clean-cut and handsome. He was an advocate for civil rights, had gotten the student government to support several protests, and hadn't been afraid to work with radicals like Felicia. After the speeches, I talked to Monica Chapman and a few others from the Fair Play committee. Like me, they suspected right-wing Cuban exiles were behind the murder. Outside the church somebody handed me a leaflet about banning the bomb.

Mr. Broussard, who had owned and lived in the building on Precita Avenue for thirty years, had already rented Felicia's apartment, and

Felicia's sister and brothers had picked up her belongings. Since the new tenant hadn't moved in yet, the landlord let me look around. He said that apart from the time his wife had died, this was the first time the police had ever been in the building. I asked him about the night Felicia had been killed, and he told me what he'd told the police. Somebody had come down the front stairs about two in the morning and had jumped the last stairs to the street.

"Did you tell the police that you'd seen me do that—jump down the stairs?" I asked.

"No, sir. I said it wasn't one of my tenants because I'm familiar with the way they go up and down the stairs." Broussard shook his head. "She was a nice girl. Maybe she got involved in something bad like drugs. Drugs are everywhere, you know. It's not safe to walk at night any more. The gangs are drug dealers. The Salvadorans hate the Nicaraguans, and they both hate the Mexicans. The 24th Street gang hates the 23rd Street gang, and they both hate the 25th Street gang."

The old man was wrong about Felicia. She'd thought drugs were sinful. In fact, she had convinced my old roommate, Charley Jessup, to get away from the drug scene in San Francisco and to stay in New York for his art studies.

I walked through the apartment, which had been freshly painted. The emptiness was painful. I went down the front stairs and studied the building from across the street. I walked to an alley that went between the buildings, made my way past garbage cans to the backyard, stepped over a low fence, climbed a second fence, and went up the rear stairway of Felicia's building. The stairs creaked. When I got to the top, I imagined Camillo waiting there. All someone would have had to do was give him treats, or just pet him, because he wasn't much of a watch dog. Then the person or persons could've entered the kitchen, crossed to the hallway, and walked a few steps to the bedroom. If Felicia had been sleeping, she'd have been easy prey. I imagined the killers creeping up the back stairs, the dog greeting them and being fed a piece of hamburger. Perhaps Felicia had heard something but decided it was only Camillo and had gone back to sleep. Then they grabbed her. Terrified, she couldn't see anyone in the dark. They took her to the bathroom. Why the bathroom? She screamed, and someone twisted her head and snapped her neck. They stood over her, watching as she slipped beneath the water. The image of them, refracted and bent by the water, would have been her last.

I went into the bathroom. According to the police, she'd probably been dragged or carried here. Why the bathroom? I knew there were ways to kill someone so that their heart would keep beating for awhile. In high school I'd been taught to stab a needle into the back of a frog's neck before cutting him open, in order to observe the beating heart. If the killer, or killers, had come up the back stairs, would they have left the way they'd come in, or would they just have gone out the front door? I remembered the front door had been unlocked when I'd arrived that morning. Now I walked to the front door and played with the lock. It was the kind that needed to be reset after the handle was turned.

On the other hand, somebody from the People's Revolutionary Party whom Felicia had met with earlier that evening—somebody she knew and trusted—might have returned with her. Or perhaps they'd met her here, at this apartment.

Assuming the police had already questioned all the neighbors, I didn't bother.

The next day Detective Mantz telephoned to ask me to come to the Hall of Justice on Bryant Street to "continue our conversation." When I told my boss, Mrs. Wilson, she asked if I wanted a lawyer. I didn't think so, but when I got to the police headquarters I was shown into a small room with Mantz and Stringfield and realized this was more than a "conversation." It was an interrogation. Again they asked me about the last time I'd seen Felicia alive. Had I been following her? Had I ever phoned her and made threats? When I asked if they'd investigated the Cuban exiles—especially the group called Cuba Libre—or if they'd talked to anyone else, they refused to tell me.

Detective Stringfield said, "Have you ever had psychiatric treatment?" How did the cops know that?

I said, "For a while, when I was a kid. Mainly I went to please my grandfather."

"Why?"

I told them what had happened in Middleground, where the Sacramento and San Joaquin Rivers merge with San Francisco Bay. "I was fourteen," I said. "Fishing by myself from a motor boat. I ran onto a sand bar. I jumped over the side to push off, but I didn't bother to turn off the motor and the boat got away from me. I swam and chased it until I was too tired to go any farther, then I sat on another sand bar. The shore was too far to reach." I'd watched as the tide had come in and begun to cover the sand bar. The sky had clouded over, so I couldn't see the shore, and I'd had the feeling of being in the middle of the ocean. I'd been terrified. Fortunately another fisherman had rescued me, but I'd been shaken up for quite a while.

"What exactly was your psychological problem?" Detective Stringfield leaned towards me.

"I didn't want to go near water, even swimming pools. For a while I couldn't even take a bath or a shower. I took sponge baths."

"How long did this go on?"

"A year or so."

"And then? You had to go for more treatments later, isn't that right?"

"I almost drowned again. What's this got to do with Felicia?"

"You have this thing about water. They call it a phobia."

"I used to. I don't now."

"Did you and Felicia Vasquez ever bathe together?"

We had, one night at Big Sur Hot Springs. There were pools on the cliffs overlooking the ocean.

Finally, after going through my history of being afraid of water and then answering questions about my friends or my lack thereof, I was allowed to leave. As I left, Detective Mantz said maybe I should write about the great baths I'd taken instead of accusing the police of protecting arsonists. I said maybe he should be out looking for Felicia's killer instead of wasting time. When I got home I called my father to ask if he'd told the police about my problems with water. He admitted having talked to the police about me, then asked how much money I was making. He laughed when I told him, and reminded me he'd gone only to the eighth grade but was making more than I, with my college education, ever would. Finally he cautioned me about making myself into a public spectacle and hurting my brother's career as well as the family name.

I told Mrs. Wilson about the police questioning and about the threats and the FBI letters Felicia and her family had received. I'd written a draft for an article about Felicia. Although it wasn't complete—I was only beginning to dig into the mystery of her death—I wanted to publish it. Mrs. Wilson gave me the go-ahead. In this article I called Felicia's "assassination" a vicious, cowardly act carried out by "fascistic perverts" who had virtually left their calling card. This was a ridiculous thing to say, but I wanted to be provocative. I ended with an invitation for people to carry on Felicia's work by defying the State Department's ban on travel to Cuba. I wrote that Americans should visit Cuba to see for themselves what Castro and Guevara were doing. "Go and see what your government doesn't want you to see," I said. "Don't be intimidated by the FBI or by gusanos."

When I wrote this, I had no idea of the consequences the article would have. The letters we received either vilified me for my pro-Cuba stance or praised me for it. And the San Francisco police invited me to the Hall of Justice for another conversation. I assumed they wanted to know what I meant by writing that Felicia's murderers had left their calling card.

This time, seated in a chair by Detective Stringfield's desk, I was shown a photograph. It was the photo I'd taken of Felicia at Big Sur, the photo which had been tacked to the wall in her bedroom. I told them the story and asked where he'd gotten it.

"We found it in her things," the policeman said, "along with this." He held up another picture. It was Felicia, lying on a beach.

"So?"

Stringfield stared at me. Mantz, the fat cop, turned in his swivel chair. His pants were tight against his crotch, outlining his genitals. He smiled at me. "You like to take pictures of girls, kid?"

"This one"—I pointed to the one of her standing on the cliff at Big Sur—"was on the wall in her bedroom. It was her favorite. The other one was taken at Aquatic Park."

The detectives stared at me.

"What did you mean in your newspaper story about a calling card?" Mantz said.

I explained that this was only journalistic rhetoric, and that I'd meant it only in a general way—that Cuban exiles or some other political cretins had killed Felicia. Mantz then advised me not to leave the Bay Area without checking first with the police.

I left the Hall of Justice thinking about the photographs. When I got home I dug out my own copies as well as other photos I had of Felicia. I got drunk that night. I couldn't sleep. I remembered the time I'd jumped from a drawbridge into the Sacramento River, to impress a few kids and no doubt to prove to myself that I wasn't afraid. I hadn't realized how high the bridge was, and I'd gone down and was still going down when my breath ran out. As I finally fell asleep, I remembered the cold and the darkness and my fear.

4

The other significant response to my article came a few days later. It was a phone call from a woman named Christina Ward, who said that she belonged to a group called the Committee to Uphold the Right to Travel (CURT), and that they were planning a trip to Cuba and would be having a public meeting. She invited me to this meeting. I asked her if the People's Revolutionary Party was involved in this committee. They were one of the supporting groups, she said.

I arrived on the Cal campus and found seven people sitting in the lecture hall that Christina had specified. At noon a woman with dark brown hair, almond-shaped eyes, and the figure and dress of a cheerleader came into the room. I wondered if she was lost—perhaps she thought this was a sorority. When it was apparent no one else was coming, the fellow with wire-rimmed glasses I'd met at the office of the People's Revolutionary Party introduced himself as Steven Bloomberg. He was now wearing workman's clothes. Then he introduced Christina Ward, Chairperson of the Committee to Uphold the Right to Travel. At this point the 'cheerleader' stood up. In the accent of an East Coast finishing school, she spoke for half an hour about our government's violation of the democratic right to travel. As she spoke, I was reminded of Felicia, probably because of a superficial resemblance—both women were beautiful and leftists. However, unlike Felicia, Christina Ward's speech was full of leftist rhetoric. I liked the voice but not the rhetoric. When she stopped for questions, I asked what the relationship was between this trip and the Cuba trip which had been initiated by Felicia Vasquez.

"We're a different group, but we have similar goals. As Americans we should have the right to see Cuba for ourselves and make up our own minds about the Revolution." She was repeating herself for at least the tenth time.

After the meeting I took a few pictures. Then Steven Bloomberg invited me to a "little gathering" the group was giving that night.

"You can talk to Christina there if you like," Bloomberg said, and now I remembered not just that I'd seen him before but that Felicia had once mentioned him. This was the fellow who had written her about carrying the collected works of Lenin wherever she went. The story Felicia told was that she'd bought the *Collected Works of V. I. Lenin* at a sale, but since she was moving to a new apartment, she'd left the books in her car. In the meantime she'd given a few rides to this fellow, Steve Bloomberg, and months later she'd gotten a letter from him saying that he now understood why she always carried the collected works of Lenin wherever she went.

The "gathering" was in the Berkeley Hills at a house owned by the Markells, whom I'd seen on campus a few times. I arrived about nine, and Loren Markell, a boyish man in his fifties who was famous as a former child prodigy and an outstanding mathematician, greeted me at the door. Tanya Markell, his wife, a short woman with frizzy hair, handed me a bottle of beer and started telling me about Fidel Castro's latest speech denouncing the United States' embargo of Cuba. After a handshake, her husband returned to a conversation with a man I vaguely recognized but couldn't place. They talked about a computer program the man was devising for dialectical logic. I went into the living room.

Christina Ward looked striking in her African dress and colorful head kerchief. She was still attractive, but different. I watched her talking to Arthur Sparrow, whom I knew as a lawyer for civil rights demonstrators. It was noisy in the house. The Ray Charles music and all the talking would make any interview, or even much of a conversation, difficult. There were a few other people I knew, including BJ Johnson, the former student body president who had spoken at Felicia's memorial, and Richard Thornton, an advocate of Black Nationalism. I sipped my beer and watched people dance. Then Steve Bloomberg approached me. Now wearing a short-sleeved white shirt, a tie, and slacks, he had blonde, curly hair and sharp features, and when he spoke, he leaned so close I could smell the mint mouthwash on his breath. I was tempted to tell him that I carried the collected works of Lenin everywhere I went, but I refrained.

"I liked your article," he said. "By the way, this is BJ Johnson. He's joining our trip."

Johnson shook my hand. It was easy to see how this handsome, friendly guy had been elected student body president the previous year. I thanked him for his speech at Felicia's memorial.

"And our next city councilman, Dick Thornton," Bloomberg said. Thornton was a huge man. He crushed my hand in his own.

"If I run," Thornton said. A few months earlier I'd seen him perform an incredible act of demagogic ju-jit-su when he'd stopped a march of angry protesters from confronting a line of Oakland cops. He'd shouted that no force on earth could stop their march. Then, with a combination of defiance, humor, appeals to morality, and clichés, he'd done a reverse and convinced the crowd that in spite of police provocations, they were going to sit down where they were and "Not Be Moved"—at which point his audience, believing they had won the battle, had started singing, and the crisis had been averted. But what were Thornton's principles? Mrs. Wilson at the *Free Express* thought he was an opportunist. I wondered what his connection was to the People's Revolutionary Party.

"We're expecting slanted coverage by the major newspapers," Bloomberg said. "We're looking for a fair-minded reporter to go on the trip with us."

I had wanted to go on Felicia's trip, and I was still curious about Cuba, but Bloomberg's invitation took me by surprise. He continued. The reporter who came on their trip would have exclusive coverage of the group's visit, the cooperation of the Cubans, no censorship, and all his expenses would be covered.

I said, "Is the Committee to Uphold the Right to Travel a front group for the People's Revolutionary Party?"

Bloomberg didn't blink. "We're an independent group. But some of us are members of the PRP."

I wanted to ask Bloomberg more questions, but this wasn't the time. I said I'd have to talk to my boss about going to Cuba. Bloomberg then said he wanted to introduce me to a few other people who were "on board."

One of these people turned out to be Frank Vara, who had been talking to Loren Markell when I'd arrived, and whom I now recognized as the man I'd seen meeting with Cantinflas, the arsonist I'd followed from the Cuba Libre office. Did this mean that Frank Vara was joining—or infiltrating—the Committee for Free Travel as an agent for right-wing Cuban exiles?

I was next introduced to Arthur Sparrow, the lawyer. In his early thirties, Sparrow was overweight and losing hair. He wore Levis and a tweed jacket, and looked more like a grad student than a lawyer.

"And you already know Christina, the chairperson of our committee," Bloomberg said.

"So glad you could come." Christina Ward shook my hand.

"I think you'll be interested to know they've eliminated racism in Cuba," Bloomberg said.

"I want to see how they did that." This was Richard Thornton.

I said I'd like to interview Ward for my newspaper. When she agreed, I got her phone number. Then she nodded and moved off. As suddenly as I'd been surrounded by people, I now found myself standing alone. There were blacks hovering around Richard Thornton, a group of women around Frank Vara, and a third group, including Bloomberg and BJ Johnson, following Christina Ward. As I watched Tanya and Loren Markell and a few others dance, I wondered if Felicia's murderers were in this room, and if I'd just shaken hands with one or more of them. Finishing my beer, I headed for the door. A tweed jacket followed me out. It was the lawyer, Art Sparrow. He stopped in the front garden and lit his pipe.

"I didn't expect to see you here," Sparrow said. "I supose your interest is because of Felicia Vasquez. I read your piece in the *Free Express*."

"Are you a member of this group?" I didn't say which group I meant.

Sparrow shook his head.

"What do you make of them?"

Sparrow took a deep breath. His moves, like his speech, were slow and deliberate. "The People's Revolutionary Party or the Committee to Uphold the Right to Travel?"

"Either. Both."

"I'd say there are a lot of big egos in one room."

"And you're going to Cuba?"

"I'm interested in Cuba," Sparrow said. "And, of course, I believe in the right to travel." He sucked on his pipe. "They're using the democratic issue, the right to travel, hypocritically. Bloomberg and Ward don't say anything about the lack of democratic rights in Cuba. What about you? Are you interested in the trip?"

I shrugged. "Do you know what the relationship was between these people and Felicia Vasquez?"

"I don't think they got along. Of course, she'd been a member of the PRP. And she was friends with their National Secretary. But I think the PRP was furious when Felicia beat them to Cuba and got an official invitation to bring a group of students. By the way, in your article you implied that Cuban exiles might have killed her. Do you know something the police don't?"

"Just trying to stir the pot."

Sparrow nodded. At this point Frank Vara came out of the house. Looking at us, he said something in Spanish I couldn't hear but which sounded threatening.

"Was that for you or for me?" I asked.

"Me," the lawyer said. "Vara takes politics very seriously. I'm just a liberal, and he doesn't like liberals."

Driving home, I tried to keep straight the various people I'd met. And I wondered about people who, as Art Sparrow said, "took politics seriously." What did that mean?

When the police wanted to question me for the fourth time, I called Art Sparrow, because he was the only lawyer I knew. My boss, Mrs. Wilson, offered to pay him, but Sparrow agreed to help me free of charge.

This time the questioning went on all afternoon. At one point the police played a tape of a phonecall. On the tape, a voice—I couldn't tell if it was male or female—said, "Your trip is cancelled."

"What did you that mean by that?" Detective Mantz said.

But I hadn't made this call and had no idea who had.

The police let me go, but again reminded me to check with them before leaving the Bay Area. Art Sparrow said it was clear that I was a suspect, perhaps their only one.

As thanks for his help, I took Sparrow to one of my favorite family-style restaurants in North Beach. Over dinner I asked him about the tape the police had played for us.

"The cops obviously thought that was your voice on the tape."

"What I want to know, Art, is who was tapping Felicia's phone? The FBI? The CIA? Because whoever was taping her calls heard this threat. Doesn't that mean they could've protected her, or at least warned her?"

"Your trip is cancelled—in retrospect it sounds like it might be a threat. But maybe it didn't at the time."

"Why didn't she tell me?"

"Maybe she thought you made the call."

"Art, we were lovers. And best friends. Who would want to cancel her trip except right-wing Cuban exiles?"

"Maybe the People's Revolutionary Party."

"Or the FBI?"

"The government doesn't go around killing people, Dante. You've been reading too much of that Kennedy conspiracy crap." The lawyer looked at me as if I were a lunatic. "Have you thought any more about going to Cuba? If you join the trip, I'll have somebody to play chess with."

"How did you know I play chess?"

"When I was a kid, I played in tournaments too." He took one of the books out of his coat pocket and held it up. It was a book of chess puzzles.

"Did we ever meet in a tournament?" I tried to picture Sparrow as one of the weirdo kids who used to show up at chess tournaments.

"No," he said. "But I did play Bobby Fischer once."

"Me too."

"I know. He beat us both."

Having been burned once by the cops, I hadn't told them about Frank Vara, whom I'd seen with one of the Cuban arsonists and at the party in the Berkeley Hills. To get an address for Vara I had to call Steve Bloomberg and tell some lies. But the result was worth it. Vara lived on Precita Avenue, two doors away from Felicia's building. I went to visit him, but no one answered. I waited in my car and watched his building for an hour. Then I tried his neighbors. A woman named Carla, who lived across the hall from Vara, told me he was almost never home.

"I think he's a student or something," the neighbor said. "He keeps funny hours."

5

I called Christina Ward and arranged for an interview at the offices of the *Free Express*, which were in a converted butcher shop on San Pablo Avenue in Oakland. A large part of the paper's income came from the sex ads we ran at the back of the paper, and I was proofreading some of them when Christina Ward showed up at ten o'clock with BJ Johnson in tow. This day she looked like a businesswoman—hair in a bun, a tailored suit. She was still beautiful, but now in a cold, sculptural way which reminded me of Tippi Hedren in *The Birds*. She sat in a chair next to my desk and crossed her legs. Johnson sprawled his tall athletic body over a nearby chair. I wondered if the former student body president was also a member of the People's Revolutionary Party.

Ward started by paraphrasing three or four Marxist principles, as if they gave her some special insight into the mysteries of the universe. Then—before I could ask any questions, or perhaps to prevent me from asking any—she went into a long speech about Mao Tse Tung and Che Guevara, as if their theories on guerrilla warfare were the Sermon on the Mount, and as if these men were her intimate friends.

Johnson said nothing. He let Ward do all the talking.

Finally she paused, and I got to ask some questions. My first was about the relationship between this trip and Felicia's.

"We arranged this trip directly with Che Guevara," Ward said. "Jake Campbell and I were in Cuba for the fifth anniversary of the Revolution."

"Your trip is similar to the trip Felicia Vasquez had planned. But you don't work with the Fair Play Committee. Why is that?"

"We tried," she said. "We wanted to meet with Felicia, but she cancelled on us. It's very difficult to work with some people. May I ask what you know about Cuba?"

I said I remembered my anxiety during the missile crisis, and that I thought that if it had been up to Castro, we might have had World War III.

"That's crap," Johnson said, surprising me with his belligerent tone. "Do you know anything about politics?"

I didn't know if Johnson's comment was for my benefit or for Christina Ward's, since, as if looking for approval, he was glancing at her.

"I don't know much," I admitted. "I'm just trying to find out something about the Committee to Uphold the Right to Travel."

Ward smiled and told me to continue with my questions.

I asked what college she was attending. She said she wasn't presently going to school.

"How did you get involved in politics?"

"Mr. Aucielo, I thought you wanted to know about our committee. Personalities are irrelevant in politics. And my personal history is unimportant."

"But newspaper readers like personal stories," I said. "I'd also like to take pictures of both of you."

Christina Ward sighed, looked at Johnson, and said, "I was a sophomore at the University of Wisconsin when Che marched into Havana on January 1, 1959. I celebrated his victory because I'm half Puerto Rican and I identify with the Cubans. I continued to pay attention to the policies of the new government after my friends had gone back to exams, football, and parties. Is that enough personal history?"

"Fidel either had to give in to the U.S. monopolies or go ahead with land reform," Johnson said. "That's what Americans don't understand."

Ward nodded and said she'd made her first trip to Cuba in the summer of 1960, inspired by the enthusiasm of the campesinos. When she'd returned home, she joined the People's Revolutionary Party. "We're a new party, more in tune with the needs of the American worker. At first I wanted to be a guerrilla fighter. But the Cubans said the best thing a North American could do to further the Revolution was return to the United States and work here—which means other kinds of revolutionary work, like what we're doing now."

"So you don't think guerrilla warfare is appropriate to this country?"

"Not at this point."

"When did you begin organizing this trip to Cuba?"

"We've been planning it for a long time. But it wasn't until Jake

Campbell and I went to Cuba in January that our plans took definite shape. The Cubans want better relations with the United States."

"When you talked to the Cubans, didn't they mention this other trip?"

"The Fair Play for Cuba Committee trip? Felicia's group? It didn't come up."

Johnson said, "The Cubans welcome everyone who's trying to help them. They would like lots of trips by Americans."

I now asked both of them about their family backgrounds, where they'd grown up.

"I'm originally from New York City," Ward said. "My father is a professor in Puerto Rico. My mother's a teacher—Irish and conservative. She disowns me for my support of Cuba."

"And your father?"

"He supports the Cuban Revolution."

"What about you, BJ?"

"You could say I'm a progressive."

Seeing I wasn't going to get much personal information, I asked what kinds of responses they were getting at the colleges they'd been to.

"American students are into their careers, not education," Christina Ward said. "Brainwashed by the media and government propaganda. For them the Third World exists as something they see occasionally on television. Americans wish the Third World, the wretched of the earth, would just go away."

"They're complacent and know nothing about history, even their own," Johnson said. "But this will change as capitalism, in its drive for profits, destroys the vaunted American standard of living."

I made notes although I had no intention of using these propaganda speeches in my article. Then I asked how their group had gotten Richard Thornton to go on the trip.

Ward said, "One difference between our trip and the one Felicia Vasquez was organizing is that she wanted only students. We'd like to have a representative group of Americans, including clergymen, artists, teachers, professionals, and politicians."

"You get the idea," Johnson said. "Crissy, I've got to get going."

I thought I had enough for my article. I was hungry and asked

Ward to join me for lunch. We drove separately and met at Brennan's on University Avenue. Compared to the other diners, Christina Ward looked like a fashion model. I drank beer with my sandwich. Christina didn't drink. As we ate, she told me how her committee was expanding. Lawrence Ferlinghetti, she said, wasn't available, but he had suggested a poet named Tim Rodman and a local artist, Earl Benton. Kenneth Rexroth, however, was hostile. He called the Committee to Uphold the Right to Travel a bunch of Stalinist hacks. Father something-or-other, a Maryknoll priest, was receptive to the idea, but said he'd have to clear it with his superiors. Bernard Holbrook, a U.C. physicist who regularly marched to ban nuclear weapons, was also interested.

"Dr. Holbrook is really weird," Ward said. "I had coffee with him at his house. There were blackboards covered with mathematical formulas in his kitchen! He was trying to explain something about quantum mechanics."

I said Holbrook was a big name in physics. With him and these artists, her trip would be more of a celebrity tour.

"We still need an independent journalist," she said.

I didn't want to appear too eager to accept this invitation, and changed the subject. "Is this your first visit to the Bay Area?"

"No. I've been here before. But you didn't answer me. What about Cuba?"

"I'll let you know. Tell me more about yourself. I mean before you became a radical."

"I traveled a lot growing up. I've lived in Buenos Aires, which San Francisco reminds me of. I've also lived in Montreal, Frankfurt… Seville. My father taught in those places, you see. It was a fairy-tale childhood. I learned languages instead of making friends. In a sense I studied the world instead of living in it. In some ways I'm still a tourist at heart."

As she continued, I didn't know what to make of her story. Her family, she said, had been poor, and they had been rich. They had lived like gypsies, and they had hobnobbed with the upper classes. She'd studied ballet, art, literature, and then she'd discovered the "truth" in Cuba. I listened. When I asked questions, her answers sounded a bit phony, as if she'd memorized them from an old movie. I could imagine Katherine

Hepburn in the part. Finally I brought up some of the things Felicia had passionately discussed—issues which, according to her, separated various revolutionary tendencies. I asked Christina what she thought of Kronstadt—meaning the Kronstadt Rebellion against the Bolshevik government after the Revolution.

"That's one place I haven't been," Christina Ward said, and laughed with a mischevious twinkle in her eyes. "Seriously, who cares if the sailors were or were not counter-revolutionary?"

I mentioned Lenin's ban on factions during the Civil War, another subject Felicia had gone on and on about. But Christina didn't care much about this issue either. I wondered if what she didn't talk about was as important as what she did. She didn't talk about what revolution might mean for actual human beings—working people, the poor, the oppressed—the people Felicia had talked about constantly. Christina referred only in passing to "the wretched of the earth," and I wondered if people existed for her only as abstractions.

"Tell me about Jacob Campbell," I said, hoping to move closer to the subject I was really interested. "What's he like?"

"Jake is the Lenin of America." Christina Ward said this with a straight face. "He's brilliant. The American Left was withering, dying out because of the McCarthy witch hunts. Jake has single-handedly revived interest in socialist ideas in America."

"How did he do that?"

"By going to the colleges and organizing support for Cuba, by organizing support for coal miners, by organizing support for civil rights."

I hadn't heard of any great socialist revival or of any recent coal strikes or of any role the People's Revolutionary Party was playing in the Civil Rights Movement. Again I asked about Felicia Vasquez.

"She was West Coast," Christina said. "I'm East Coast. As I told you over the phone, I read what you wrote about her. It was quite moving. I liked the anger you showed in your article. You implied that you know more about who killed her than has come out. What did you mean?"

I shook my head and shrugged.

"Do you think it was gusanos?"

"If it was, the police are protecting them. Nobody's even been arrested for the fire at the Fair Play for Cuba Office. Felicia got threatening letters. But the cops don't seem interested in them."

"The FBI was probably threatening her themselves. Our offices have been attacked too. Anyone who supports Cuba is harassed by the government, or by Cuban exile groups funded by our government."

"The police say the last people to see her alive were people from your organization," I lied.

"That's not true." I'd struck the wrong note and been caught. Ward stood up. "The last people to see her alive were the people who killed her. I have to go."

Outside the restaurant I said, "Why do you want me to go on your trip? My newspaper has a tiny circulation."

"The regular press will either blank us out or tell lies. But we have a few connections. So do the Cubans. Your articles, if they're good, would be circulated all over Latin America."

As she drove away, I wondered about the "connections" of the People's Revolutionary Party.

At home that night, I picked up *Our Man in Havana*. I liked the game of checkers in this story. After taking an opponent's piece, which is a miniature bottle of scotch or bourbon, Mr. Wormold and Captain Segura must drink their capture. I tried to imitate their game by replaying an old game of chess from a book and drinking a shot of whisky after each move. When I could no longer focus on the board, I tried to sleep, but my thoughts kept going to Christina Ward. I awoke in the middle of the night and reached out to touch Camillo. Since coming to live with me, the dog always slept next to my bed. But he wasn't there. I heard something in the next room. What was he doing? I called, but he didn't come. I called again. Now I saw that the bedroom door had somehow closed, and the dog was locked in the next room. I got up to open it. I must've drunk more than I thought because I'd left the lights on. Camillo wasn't in this room either. I went into the kitchen, but the dog wasn't there. I found him trapped in the bathroom. I couldn't remember what I'd been doing, but I'd left photos of Felicia spread out on the floor.

When I went back to sleep I had another dream about her. In the dream she came close and looked into my eyes. She was so beautiful that I ached. Except for the tears I'd shed at the cemetery when she was buried, I didn't remember the last time I'd cried, but now I awoke sobbing. The sobs came in waves. I was wracked with them until I finally fell asleep.

6

Mrs. Wilson was all for me going to Cuba, especially since the trip wouldn't cost her newspaper anything. I said I could work on various stories—the Cuban Revolution, of course, and the People's Revolutionary Party, and perhaps something about Cuban exiles. But my main interest, which I didn't tell Mrs. Wilson, was still learning the truth about Felicia's murder.

"I've met the old bird who started the People's Revolutionary Party," Mrs. Wilson said. "His name's Tom Kinkaid. He's retired out in Walnut Creek. He thinks the way to build a progressive movement is to put kids into situations where they get their heads bashed in by the police. Then his party might recruit one or two of the dumber ones. Kinkaid himself is an alcoholic. I think they keep him alive so that the new leaders can drag him out once in a while to help raise money. Kinkaid claims to have known Eugene V. Debs, Big Bill Haywood, and some of the other famous wobblies and commies. Anyway, be careful of these people. They play rough. But… if you're really serious about going to Cuba, look up the recent speeches of Che Guevara. He's the real thing, Dante. He's been saying things no Communist has had the guts to say in a long time. The Soviets support Cuba economically, but their line of peaceful co-existence means using foreign revolutionaries for Russia's own purposes. Guevara, however, calls for world revolution. The question is where Fidel stands. Either Castro has to go with the Russians or with Guevara, but he can't have it both ways."

From the office I phoned Christina Ward to tell her I was accepting her invitation to go to Cuba. Driving home, I had the feeling I was being followed. I didn't see anyone—or rather, I saw too many people who looked suspicious. I was getting paranoid, and the trip hadn't even begun.

The next day Paul Larson, the FBI agent who had accompanied Detectives Mantz and Stringfield, visited me at my apartment and brought with him a Dr. Marcus. Marcus, like Larson, was tall, and his gray hair was also trimmed in a crew cut.

"To what do I owe this visit?" I asked.

"Do you plan to make journalism your career?" Dr. Marcus said.

"I don't know. Why?"

"What are your plans?"

"I don't have any. I'm a free spirit, the last of the beatniks."

"What did you study in school?"

"A little of this and a little of that."

"You don't remember what you majored in?"

"Philosophy. Why?"

"Have you ever been arrested?"

"No."

"Your friend Charles Jessup was arrested while you were roommates for petty theft—shoplifting—and then for check kiting. He opened an account at the Bank of America for one thousand dollars, then accounts at Wells Fargo, Crocker, Pacific, and First National. For several weeks he moved various amounts of his original one thousand dollars between these banks, and then, within one hour, he hit them all for a withdrawal of a thousand dollars. And he did all this under your name."

"I wasn't involved, as you must surely know."

"If your grandfather hadn't bailed Jessup out and made good on the money so that nobody pressed charges, both of you might have gone to prison."

"Charley admitted he'd stolen my identification." Of course I knew why my friend had done this. He'd been desperate for drug money.

"When you worked for the Alameda County Welfare Department," Dr. Marcus continued, "you were responsible for three thousand two hundred and eighty dollars in overpayments to your clients."

This was probably the amount of extra vouchers I'd sent people who'd run out of money before the end of the month. I didn't think what I'd done was illegal, but I was surprised the FBI had taken such an interest in me that they'd gone to the trouble to find this out.

"And when you worked in a loan office you contacted various people who had skipped out on their debts and told them your company knew where they worked or lived, and that they should move or get new jobs."

Where had he gotten such information? I didn't think anyone had known about my little acts of sabotage at the loan company.

"I mention these things, Mr. Aucielo, so that we all know where we stand. The reason I'm here is that I have contacts with the Voice of America, and I thought you, as a journalist, might be interested in working for them in Europe. The money would be a substantial increase over what you're earning now, plus extra money to cover the costs of living abroad. Besides that, your passport will not be confiscated if you go to Cuba, nor will you face fines or imprisonment when you come back."

I stared at the FBI agent.

He said, "You've been invited on this illegal trip to Cuba by the People's Revolutionary Party, and you've accepted their offer. Write your stories." He smiled. "And take your pictures."

"Who reads the *Free Express* anyway?" the other agent, Larson, said. "But you might go easy on this Felicia Vasquez business. Of course, if you learn something about her death, fine. Castro's people were probably involved."

"We'll discuss that when you get back," Marcus said, "along with any other information you pick up. We know you have an excellent memory, mental chess and so forth. And any photos you get could be helpful."

"You want me to be a spy?" As a kid I'd fantasized about being a spy, and often even thought of myself as one. Now that I actually had an offer, I felt sick.

The agents glanced at each other. Larson said, "You were concerned about the death of one person, Felicia Vasquez. In relation to the deaths of thousands of people—because that's what Castro's regime has on its hands—you shouldn't have any qualms."

"Can I have this offer in writing?" I didn't think anyone would ever believe me, and I thought this would make a fine newspaper story.

"You'll have to trust us," Marcus said.

Larson said, "You'll be dealing with hardcore people in an enemy country. A country which, by the way, grants its citizens none of the freedoms we enjoy here."

"My girlfriend had her telephone tapped and her conversations recorded," I said. "My guess is that you people did that. You recorded threats to her, but you didn't give her any protection. When I told the police about Cuba Libre and where to find the gusanos who torched the Fair Play for Cuba office, suddenly these Cuban fascists disappeared. I want to know, now, what you're doing to catch the people who killed Felicia Fasquez. When you've caught them, then we'll have something to talk about."

"The Vasquez case is a San Francisco police matter," Larson said. "And by the way, don't forget to tell Detective Mantz that you're taking this trip."

"I guess you're tapping my phone now too," I said, "and my newspaper's. So you can tell fatso and stringbean I'm leaving town for awhile. And you can find out what I have to say about Cuba in the *Free Express*. I'll be sending in articles from Havana."

Mrs. Wilson said she'd contacted the Emergency Civil Liberties Union, who would defend me if the government tried to take my passport. She'd also contacted the press services, which might distribute some of my articles and photos.

"Do I need to get permission for this trip from the San Francisco police?"

Mrs. Wilson checked with her lawyer, who said I didn't. I also called Art Sparrow, who said he'd take care of this for me and that he'd bring his portable chess set for the plane.

I needed the *Free Express* to supply me with at least one more camera and plenty of film.

Mrs. Wilson agreed. I got two cameras, a Rolaflex 120 with tons of film, a tripod stand, and an automatic timer so that I could leave this camera in place, for example in front of a podium when someone was speaking. Then I'd be able to move around and get other shots with the Leica M3 she also gave me, or with my own Nikon F. So I was well-equipped.

Steve Blomberg informed me I'd be driving to New York City in a rental car with five other people. From New York we'd fly to Cuba by way of a third country. I telephoned Charley Jessup, my old roommate, and asked if I could stay with him while I was in New York. Then I told him about the Cuban exiles, the People's Revolutionary Party, and my dealings so far with the police and the FBI.

The exiles were vicious, I told him. They were probably financed by the U.S. government, but were certainly protected by it. They'd vandalized Fair Play for Cuba, sent threatening notes to Felicia, and may have killed her. And one of their people, Frank Vara, lived close to Felicia's apartment, had probably been watching her, and was going to Cuba on this trip. According to Bloomberg, Vara was one of the people I'd be driving across the country with. Hopefully I'd be able to learn more about him as well as the organizers of the trip, the People's Revolutionary Party and its front group, the Committee to Uphold the Right to Travel, which had been in conflict with Felicia's planned trip. The PRP denied having met with Felicia the night she was killed. I needed to know if that meeting had taken place or not. Anne Montrose, a member of the PRP who might have knowledge of that meeting, would also be driving across the country with me. BJ Johnson, the former student body president and a co-chair of the Committee, would be in the car, as would Monica Chapman, who had known Felicia in the Fair Play committee. I didn't know anything about the other person.

This would be a very interesting drive across the United States.

Before I left, we struck a deal with the Associated Press to send my stories and photos from the Prensa Latina office in Havana to the AP office in Mexico City. AP would have first rights and would deal with Mrs. Wilson. If I got any special photos—Castro, Guevara, particularly newsworthy events—I'd send the negatives by plane to Mexico City, where they'd be sent on to New York or San Francisco.

I left the dog, Camillo, to take care of my grandfather.

7

This was the first time I'd crossed the United States—in a car with five other people, one of whom might be a murderer. Clifton Specks, an unkempt but friendly guy, was the only person I knew nothing about. Anne Montrose, a short, attractive woman, was a member of the People's Revolutionary Party. The others—BJ Johnson, Frank Vara, and Monica Chapman—I'd already met. I'd had been expecting grandeur, like on the postcards, but the transcontinental highway gave a different picture of the country—mile after mile of desert, rocky hillsides that made me think of a dead planet, towns and cities that, if their names weren't posted, I couldn't have told apart. Instead of canyons, mountains, forests, and valleys, I discovered an endless stream of trucks, trailers, cars, billboards, patches of refuse and garbage, scrap heaps, junked automobiles, car parts turning to rust, and signs announcing "historical sites" just a few miles farther along. Sinclair Lewis's Main Street and even F. Scott Fitzgerald's ash heap seemed like romantic dreams.

As soon as the drive began, paranoia emerged. No doubt each of the others had also been approached by FBI agents, so each of us was suspicious. Only Clifton Specks, grossly obese but always smiling, was not suspected of being an agent, at least by me. For one thing, he was too dirty. He smelled so bad that an hour out of Berkeley, Johnson and Frank Vara insisted that we pull into a service station and force Specks to wash and put on clean clothes. While we were waiting for him, Anne Montrose explained that Specks hadn't been like this when he was interviewed for the trip. Then he had claimed to be a psychology student at San Francisco State College.

Frank Vara, who claimed to be a "Fidelista," began flirting with Anne Montrose. When she didn't respond to his advances, he tried Monica, who wore only the skimpiest of blouses, and whose short skirts revealed well-tanned, well-shaped legs. I now learned that she was an art student and the daughter of a real-estate millionaire. Monica might be flirting with radical politics, but she was not interested in flirting with Vara. I caught him staring at me and wondered if he suspected that I knew he was a gusano. But perhaps he was only jealous that it was my shoulder that Monica preferred to lean on when she slept.

BJ Johnson—tanned, blonde hair cut short, blue eyes sparkling—wore shorts and a T-shirt most of the time. He knew by heart the statistics of dozens of baseball players, and informed us that Fidel Castro had once been recruited by the Yankees but had chosen guerrilla warfare over baseball. Anne Montrose and Frank Vara often talked in Spanish. Hoping they might reveal something, I didn't let on that I understood. The common topic was the Kennedy assassination, which everybody believed was a conspiracy, although each of us had a different theory about who the conspirators were.

One night Monica Chapman, who had worked with Felicia in the Fair Play Committee and had been in the office when it was torched, brought up the subject of Felicia's murder. I was driving, and she was sitting next to me. I thought everyone else was sleeping, and was immediately glad I hadn't revealed my suspicions about Vara or about the People's Revolutionary Party.

"She was a nice girl," BJ said. He was in the front seat, on the other side of Monica. "And smart too. Maybe she was too trusting, you know, and let someone into her house who, you know…"

"I think it was right-wing Cuban exiles," Anne Montrose said from the back seat. "But you never know what kinds of things people are involved in. How did Felicia get to Cuba? I've always wondered about that. And how did she meet Castro and Guevara and arrange that trip she was organizing? Where did she get her money?"

BJ argued in Felicia's defense. He said there had been discussion about combining Felicia's trip with this trip. Then Clifton said he'd also known Felicia. And Frank Vara blurted out, "Maybe she ran afoul of Castro." After this, perhaps knowing he'd said too much, Vara was practically silent for the rest of the trip.

Seeing that it was impossible to have a private conversation in the car, I said nothing more about Felicia.

Three thousand miles of flat land, corn fields, suspicions, and mistrust. Once, we had to stop so that Anne could buy some clothes. She was certain she'd packed them, but they'd gotten lost.

Of course, we had to stop for food and gas. Eating in roadside cafes and bars, we drew stares. Perhaps it was our California license plates or our clothes or the way we combed our hair. Perhaps it Frank Vara's dark skin. Aware of the violence civil rights workers had encountered in the South, we kept to ourselves and observed the speed limits. But the racist comments were hard to ignore. In one restaurant, listening to a guy in a cowboy hat talking about how Cuba ought to be nuked, I had the odd thought that this was my 'troika' journey through Siberia.

We didn't stop to sleep but traded turns at the wheel and drove straight through—most of the time in silence.

8

The office of the Committee to Uphold the Right to Travel was a tenement apartment on the Lower East Side. We were greeted by a woman wearing a gray jumper, black stockings, and no make-up who introduced herself as Sharon Albright. Young men in work clothes—students, I thought, posing as "proletarians"—argued in another part of the room. Albright told us where and when to show up for the flight, but she did not give us any other details. I asked if we were we going to Cuba via Mexico or Canada. She shook her head.

"Everything's very secretive," she whispered.

Steve Bloomberg came out of another room and shook my hand. "Glad to have the press with us," he said.

I asked about Christina Ward. She was around, Bloomberg said. Then he introduced me to Lou Corbett, "an expert on the local cultural scene." Corbett was a huge bear of a man who volunteered to show me around the city, and we arranged to meet the next day. The Committee offered to put me up with "one of the comrades." Instead, I telephoned Charley Jessup and headed uptown to the address he'd given me.

As I headed for the subway, I noticed that two men in suits were following me.

Charley Jessup was now the caretaker of Lillian Hellman's house, a brownstone mansion half a block from the Metropolitan Museum. He had a separate apartment with a private entrance at the back, and he had filled it with canvases of his abstract expressionist art—none of which had ever made sense to me. Several inches shorter than I, Charley was built solidly, and with his red hair and freckles, his jokes and fun-loving nature, he seemed to me a modern version of Tom Sawyer. However, he'd lost weight, and although he assured me he was clean of drugs, his nervousness and incessant talking made me doubt him.

"Let me show you the house. Lillian knew my father. That's how I got the job. She's on vacation. Want to see the house? Let me show you the house."

I'd read Hellman's plays and knew of her relationship with Dashiell Hammett, but I hadn't realized she'd been a Communist, or at least a sympathizer. Pictures of her as a child in the South and as a young woman adorned the walls, including the walls alongside the staircase. In fact, there were photographs of her everywhere in the house. What kind of person, I wondered, would want to look at herself so much?

Charley made a list of places, like The Cloisters and Wall Street, for me to visit. Then he took me to the White Horse Tavern, "where Dylan Thomas used to drink," and then for a ride to Staten Island on the ferry. After this we had a beer in Greenwich Village and toured some of the clubs. The two men in the suits continued to tail us.

The next day I was supposed to meet Lou Corbett for another tour of New York. Instead, Jake Campbell himself showed up at the Lower East Side apartment-headquarters to tell me that our flight would be postponed. I don't know what I was expecting, but Campbell was a nondescript guy in his mid-thirties, five-ten or eleven, balding, with plain features. He could have been a grocery clerk or a car salesman. He didn't look like "the Lenin of America."

"Instead of driving non-stop across the continent, you guys could've taken your time," he said. His voice was slightly high-pitched. I saw nothing at all charismatic about him. I wondered what Felicia had ever seen, or why Christina Ward had praised him so.

"But this means you have a few extra days to tour," Campbell continued. "It's the FBI, of course. They're putting pressure on anyone who signed up for the trip. Unfortunately, they're having some success. Several people have dropped out. And it looks like we'll have to go all the way around the block to get next door."

When I asked what he meant by this, Campbell smiled.

What I wanted to see most were the museums. But Campbell's personal tour for me included Harlem, the West Side, Brooklyn, and Queens. "So that you get an idea of what this megalopolis means to the people who actually have to live in its squalid boroughs and slums and garbage-strewn streets," he said.

Throughout the tour, the two men in suits stuck with us, following about fifty yards to the rear. They looked amazingly like the FBI agents I'd already met in San Francisco. They didn't bother trying to hide the fact they were following us.

"What sins," Campbell said, ignoring the men following us, "did the people who live in these neighborhoods commit to have been consigned to such hellish lives?"

As we continued the tour, Campbell told me he'd been an economics student at the University of Chicago before joining the PRP. Then, I suppose as preparation for the trip, he gave me an introduction to Cuban history—from his own point of view. Castro, he said, in order to keep his promise to the Cuban peasants about land reform, had "inevitably" come into conflict with American economic interests, like the Hearst sugar plantations.

Campbell deliberately brought me to Times Square, to the corner of 42nd Street, where he directed me to contrast the grandeur of the sky scrapers with the poverty of a black man who stood a few feet away from us. The man had a sign—"27 years in an Alabama prison for stealing a chicken"—and held out a cup while the crowds rushed by. Campbell looked at me as if he'd just demolished any arguments I might have.

"It was inevitable," Campbell said, continuing his lecture about Cuba. "Inevitable" was a big word for this man. "The difference between Cuba and all the other so-called revolutions in Latin America, like Arbenz in Guatemala, is that Fidel disbanded the old army and police force. So when the United States refused to refine Soviet oil and froze Cuban assets in American banks, Cuba retaliated by nationalizing American companies. And this is the key point, Aucielo—there were no right-wing generals or colonels left on the island to make a coup."

As we walked, I wondered what had made this man join the People's Revolutionary Party, a tiny left-wing party that was no more than a pimple on the backside of society.

"I'm a product of the Cuban Revolution," he said. "In 1959 I was being groomed for the corporate world. Then I went to see Cuba for myself. I'd been a Republican, believe it or not. One night I met Fidel. I just walked up to him in the lobby of the Havana Hilton where he was talking with some people, and started asking questions. The next thing you know, he invited me to go fishing with him, then to stay in Cuba and work as an economist. But I knew the best way to help the Cubans was to make a revolution in the United States."

I brought up Felicia Vasquez, who had also met Castro. We were on Wall Street.

Campbell said, "I had a lot of respect for Felicia. I never understood why she left us." Then, abruptly changing the subject, he said, "Actually no one's supposed to know this. The State Department has put pressure on the Canadians and the Mexicans. We can't fly to Havana from either Montreal or Mexico City. So it looks like Paris or Madrid."

I asked how many members were in his group.

"How many did Lenin have in 1916?" Campbell said, avoiding a direct answer. "We're putting all our other work on hold in order to focus on this trip. Only a few party members will actually be going. The rest of the comrades will be organizing public meetings for when we get back."

I asked again about the relationship between this trip and the one Felicia had been organizing.

"They're entirely different concepts. Naturally the Cubans welcome any Americans who want to visit their country. Understand, there was no competition between Felicia and me. But you make enemies. It's inevitable in politics. For example, some people think you're FBI. Others think Frank Vara is. But don't pay attention to gossip. I know, and the Cubans know, that inevitably we're going to have agents on this trip."

That night Anne Montrose telephoned me while I was asleep in Charley's apartment and asked if we could meet for a drink. She was going to the Museum of Modern Art the next day and wanted me to meet her there. I asked her to call me in the morning, hung up, and went back to sleep. The phone rang again. This time Anne said it was very important. Now, unable to get back to sleep, I lay on the sofa. Finally, thinking about Felicia in Big Sur, I fell asleep. Soon after, Charley and his girlfriend came back from a night on the town. The door woke me. They passed through and disappeared into his bedroom.

I waited an hour for Anne Montrose in the museum garden. I looked at the sculptures, went inside, checked the garden again. Then, thinking she might be somewhere else in the museum, I walked around and looked at some of the art. But I couldn't concentrate. I was wondering about Campbell. Had he and maybe Steve Bloomberg or Lou Corbett been the ones standing over Felicia as she drowned? A group of people left the gallery I was in, and suddenly I was standing alone, surrounded by masterpieces but able to think only about a woman drowned in a bathtub.

Probably I'd missed Anne Montrose while I'd been wandering around. I left the museum, and, thinking I should try to learn more about the People's Revolutionary Party, I headed to the Lower West Side print shop, which the group operated. Lou Corbett—"the Bear" as he was called—let me in and gave me a tour. The place was clean and modern, and the staff looked like well-paid professionals. Corbett's pride was the party's giant new web press. The party also owned two large Harris offsets and half a dozen Multilith offset presses. Everybody in the New York chapter, including party leaders, took shifts here, although the main work was done by a full-time crew—"at union wages with union benefits." In a small lunch room, Corbett poured us each a cup of coffee.

"I'm glad you decided to join the trip," the bear said. "You know, one of our own members just caved in from the FBI threats. Anne Montrose, who was supposed to be part of our legal team."

I said I'd driven to New York with her. I didn't mention the meeting we were supposed to have had.

Corbett shook his head. "You never know about people. I suppose her career takes precedence."

No doubt this was why Anne had wanted to meet me—to talk about her decision. But why me? We hadn't been friends. On the trip across the country she'd actually been cold towards me.

"This trip—what does your group get out of it?" I asked. "I mean, besides publicity, which could be bad as well as good."

The trip to Cuba, Corbett admitted, was only partly about Cuba. The party's main goal was to recruit, to build a cadre organization. "What's at stake is this," Corbett said. "Who will lead the coming American revolution?"

I nodded, trying to project a kind of sober thoughtfulness. But inside, questions churned. Could this be why Felicia was murdered? Did Jacob Campbell think that because Castro and a dozen or so men had conquered a small island, the People's Revolutionary Party could do the same thing in the United States? How crazy were these people? How far would Jacob Campbell, I thought, go to eliminate anyone—like Felicia—whom he saw as an obstacle to this grandiose scheme?

9

Only when I got to the airport did I learn we were flying to Amsterdam. This was also the first time I got a look at our complete group. Including myself, I counted thirteen of us—the men with well-trimmed hair, in sports coats, white shirts, and ties; the women in summer dresses. We could've been a group of college students, or even a church group, leaving for a summer tour of Europe.

The first person I spotted was Frank Vara, talking to Dick Thornton, the Black Nationalist ex-preacher from Oakland. Thornton was with his girlfriend, Arlene Washington, and two men who looked like bodyguards but who were only there to see him off. Jake Campbell was surrounded by a dozen members of the People's Revolutionary Party. Monica Chapman, BJ Johnson, and Art Sparrow were talking in another cluster. Christina Ward was with Steve Bloomberg and Sharon Albright, the secretary I'd seen at the office on the Lower East Side, and a chubby woman named Helen Anderson, who would be the fifth party member on the trip. Clifton Specks stood by himself.

Before we were allowed to board the plane, an official from the State Department ushered us all into a room and told us that we would be facing arrest, loss of our passports, and fines if we traveled to Cuba. Jake Campbell responded with a short speech about the right to travel.

On the plane, I sat with Art Sparrow. Once we were in the air, he suggested we play a game of chess, but I was too excited. People began moving around, introducing themselves. Introducing myself to Thornton and his girlfriend, Arlene Washington, I said I was the reporter from the *Berkeley Free Express* and that I'd be covering the group's visit.

"We like adventure," Thornton said. "Of course, traveling together, we'll all be sharing meals and bus rides and hotels, and I assume you'll want to know my reactions, observations, questions, and criticisms. The Cubans will show us only what they want us to see, but I intend to see the real Cuba."

As Thornton talked, I noticed the first sexual pairings had begun. Steve Bloomberg was making himself known to Monica Chapman, giving her his opinions about Cuba, the Kennedy assassination, Lyndon Johnson's chances in November, the Sino-Soviet dispute, and the plight of civil rights workers in Mississippi. From the way Monica was listening to him, Bloomberg was apparently having some success. Frank Vara chatted up Sharon Albright and seemed to be watching me as I moved around the plane. BJ Johnson talked to Christina Ward.

"I know the Russians didn't make a utopia," Arlene Washington said. "But maybe the Cubans are doing better." Arlene was originally from Mississippi and was now studying sociology at Berkeley.

I hadn't seen Christina Ward since San Francisco. When we were above the mid-Atlantic I sat next to her, but she said she'd been up late and needed to sleep. After a while I felt drowsy too and closed my eyes. When I awoke, my head had fallen onto her shoulder. I apologized.

"That's okay." Christina was wearing a cashmere sweater and smelled lovely.

"I hope I didn't drool."

"You looked comfortable. Are you awake now?" I nodded. "Then can I have a turn?" Before I could answer, she leaned her head against my shoulder, snuggled against me, and seemed to fall asleep immediately. Then I fell asleep again. When I awoke, our faces were about an inch apart.

In Amsterdam we were ushered into a room before we could catch our connecting flight to Paris, and another U.S. State Department official gave us the same warning about the consequences of defying the travel ban. The group's reactions were a mixture of guffaws and silence. While we waited for our flight to Paris, I asked Christina about Frank Vara.

"He's a student," she said. "From Chile originally. These State Department flunkies are too much, don't you think?"

Then we were in Paris. An airport bus dropped us at the Quai D'Orsay, where we had a view of various monuments—the Hotel Des Invalides and the Eglise du Dome, the Grand Palais and the Petit Palais across the river, and the Alexander III bridge.

"Napoleon's Tomb," Art said, pointing up the Esplanade des Invalides, and making me realize again that there was more to history than I'd been taught in American schools.

On the way to our hotels, we took pictures through the windows of the chartered bus. I wanted to look up the only person I knew in France, Mike Pettit, a friend from college who was studying at the Sorbonne. I remembered that Felicia and I had talked about taking a trip to Paris, and I thought that perhaps after Cuba I'd come back, and hopefully Mike would put me up. After dropping off my luggage, I took a cab to Mike's address. And now I got the feeling I was in a movie, a strange farce with absurd rules. Mike's apartment was in a six-story building in a tiny alley, but he wasn't home. I went down to the sidewalk. Across the street was a bakery with a plate-glass window. As I stood in front of Mike's building, I saw my reflection in the bakery window. And there was also another reflection: two men peeking from around the corner, looking directly at me. Both men wore trenchcoats. I had to laugh—life imitating a movie, and a bad movie at that. I watched them watching me. Then I went back upstairs and left Mike a note.

It was raining when I got back to the hotel room I was sharing with Art Sparrow. The two of us went to a nearby café for a drink, talked about the trip so far and about the People's Revolutionary Party. Art said he'd heard that the PRP print shop was a sweat shop which exploited the faithful members. I said that I'd been there and hadn't seen anything like that.

"In Cuba they're going to put on a dog-and-pony show and show us what they want us to see." Art lit his pipe. "Just as Campbell no doubt put on a show for you."

"I suppose people always get taken in. Like the intellectuals who visited the Soviet Union in the twenties and thirties and came back singing the praises of Stalin."

"I know for a fact Campbell runs a sweat shop. On the surface, which is what you saw, things looks fine—union wages, nice working conditions—it's all for show, so that Campbell can put the union label on what he prints. What you didn't see is that his happy workers return most of their wages to the party."

Steve Bloomberg was staying at the same hotel as Art and I. According to Art, Bloomberg was there to keep an eye on us. Christina Ward was a few blocks away at another hotel. She telephoned and asked me to have dinner with her. Was she just being friendly, I wondered, or did she have an ulterior reason for being nice to me?

At the restaurant she talked about Paris, then about art and then about photography. I said I hoped to get some good pictures in Cuba. Christina said the Cubans would help me with supplies like developer. In spite of a drizzle, she suggested we take a walk. I had no idea where we were, but I didn't mind.

"These streets have been home to Verlaine, Balzac, Stendhal, Rimbaud, Proust, Hemingway, Picasso," she said, and pointed at an old building. "Perhaps Camus or Sartre or Renoir lived in some of these places."

I knew these names, but that was all. Christina sounded as if she'd studied their works, and I asked her about this. She just shrugged.

Fog drifted through the streets. We approached the river, crossed a bridge, and found ourselves on an island in the middle of the city. Now she was talking about the history of this city.

"I hate geometrically planned cities, don't you?" she said. "I like the fact that these narrow little streets are unsuited for cars."

I said, "When you and Jake Campbell went to Cuba to arrange this trip, how long were you there?"

"Paris had grown organically, over centuries," Christina said, as if she hadn't heard me. "American cities are always new, old buildings being torn down to make way for new ones. Streets that are all parallel and perpendicular may be practical, but they're so boring. I wonder if living in a grid conditions one's thinking. I wonder if this is why Americans make pilgrimages to Europe—to escape that grid."

"Tell me about your trip to Cuba earlier this year."

"It was quite brief. We didn't even get out of Havana." She took hold of my hand and said she didn't want to leave Paris. Right now she didn't even want to think about Cuba.

"Did you ever think about the explorers who went to the New World searching for El Dorado?" she said. "They voyaged into the unknown, when the real treasures of civilization are right here. But most people never see the beauty, even though it's often right on the surface." She stopped and looked up at one of the old buildings. "The people who live here are blinded by the routine of their lives. And people who don't live here are mostly too poor to travel."

I was trying to think of a way to get her to talk about her political agenda. I wasn't in the mood for a lecture about art or culture.

Christina said, "Let's go to the Louvre tomorrow. Will you come with me?" Then, as we turned a corner, she let go of my hand, and to my surprise we were back at her hotel. She smiled, said good night, and dashed inside, leaving me on an empty street.

I was supposed to meet her at eleven. When I learned the museum opened earlier, I telephoned her. She wasn't in her room, so I walked over to her hotel. As I approached, I saw Christina heading away from me. I picked up my pace to catch her, but before I could, she was joined by a tall man. After two blocks they went into a café. I decided to follow them inside.

"I was just passing by and saw you," I said.

As if she'd been expecting me, Christina smiled and introduced me to her friend.

"This is Paul Bertrand," she said. The man had a blonde mustache and blonde, almost white hair. He was young, in his early thirties at most, and wore a dark suit which looked a bit threadbare, and thin loafers.

"Paul is my comrade," Christina said. "He's one of our European co-thinkers. He wants me to write about our trip for his journal."

Coffee was served, and Christina and her comrade began speaking in rapid-fire French. I could pick up a word here and there, but I had no idea what they were talking about. Then they switched to German. Christina turned to me.

"Please excuse us," she said. "Paul's English is not good. I told him you're also a journalist and photographer and might be interested in contributing to his journal."

I shrugged.

Christina and Paul Bertrand talked for another few minutes. Then Bertrand got up, shook my hand, kissed Christina on the cheek, and left without asking for a way to contact me or giving me a way to contact him. I mentioned this to Christina on our way back to the museum. Christina said this was because she already had the address of his journal. On the way to the Louvre we passed by a theater playing an old Gary Cooper movie.

"It's *The Train Whistles Three Times*," she said. "Have you seen it?"

"The posters look like *High Noon*," I said.

"Of course," she said. "*High Noon*."

After a quick tour of the museum, we sat at a sidewalk café and talked about some of the pictures.

"But I think the real beauty of Paris is in the streets," Christina said. "In the colors and the crowds and the old buildings, the trees and the gardens, the river and canals, even the pissoirs."

"There probably won't be much of this in Cuba," I said, pointing to the pastry we were eating.

"Let's stay here, you and me. We'll live in a garret," she said, smiling. She was quite beautiful. Before I could say anything, she said, "But Paris has been here a long time. I love it, but we must also think about the society that produced all this. Its history is a history of carnage, and Cuba stands for a world where everyone, not just the rich, will participate in art."

Before leaving Paris, I tried again to reach my friend Mike Pettit. He never did answer the note I'd left at his apartment. I didn't learn why until much later.

Our next stop was Czechoslovakia. From there we were scheduled to take a Cubana Airlines flight to Havana. The farms and fields we flew over on the way to Prague seemed to me bleached out and faded. Then, in just a couple of hours, we were behind the Iron Curtain.

10

Surveillance at the Prague airport was of another order, as absurd as Frenchmen in trench coats peeking at me from around a corner, but somehow not as comic. This was a cold place—soldiers, men and women in dark suits, everyone watching us as we were herded from the plane onto a bus. We would not wander around this city as we'd wandered around Paris, but were driven directly to a border town called Carlovivari, or Carlsbad, formerly a spa for the rich, now a proletarian resort. The colorful bustle of the Parisian streets was gone. Central European mountains and castles brooded dreamily in the distance.

We stayed in the Grand Moskva Hotel to await the Cubana Airliner which would take us back across the Atlantic. Carlsbad looked like a fairy tale which had become a bit seedy. The dining rooms and stairways, built as monuments to nineteenth-century wealth, felt oppressive, and even the bathtub in my bathroom—the size of a small swimming pool, with marble steps going into the tub—seemed uninviting. I called Christina to ask if she wanted to go for a walk. She said she had a meeting.

On our first afternoon, BJ Johnson and I set out to explore the surrounding hills, two young, wide-eyed Americans. But we hadn't gone far when it began to rain, so we hurried down the hillside, found a tavern, and went in for a beer. Since I hadn't really had a chance to talk to BJ alone, I asked him now if he was a member of the People's Revolutionary Party.

"No, no," he said. "But I'll work with anybody if we've got the same goal. I'm not prejudiced." He smiled his infectious smile. "Felicia was a member. But you knew that. I worked with her too."

"Did you know her very well?"

"We went to a movie once, but we were with a whole crowd so I wouldn't exactly call it a date. She was always so serious and dedicated that I felt immature, even superficial, around her." He shrugged. I thought this guy could probably have any women he wanted. I'd already seen Sharon Albright flirting with him. "You know, Felicia reminded me of a girl I knew in third grade. This particular girl was a very good artist. All of us kids would crowd around her desk and watch her draw, and we'd ask her to put a bird here, or a tree there, and she would. She was like a little mother. I loved her, but more like a mother. Felicia had that quality. I worked with her on a few projects, a civil rights demonstration and some fund-raising to send people to register black voters in the South."

"BJ, what do you know about Frank Vara?"

"Frank? He seems like a nice guy. You know, Frank and I are both thinking about staying in Cuba or coming back later, maybe through Mexico. I'd like to help build schools and stuff."

Because the hotel restaurant was so oppressive, that night Art and I went out to look for another place to eat. We were walking along the river, not in any rush, and as we stood on a corner wondering which direction to go in, BJ joined us.

"I saw you guys from the other side of the river," he said. "I can't eat at that hotel. The food's terrible, and the place is too dark. Mind if I join you?"

The three of us walked on. I spotted Christina, sitting in a tavern with an older man with gray hair and a handlebar mustache. She saw us and waved for us to join her. She introduced her companion as Jan Hutoc. Mr. Hutoc had overheard her and Jake Campbell speaking English and had introduced himself. Jake had to go back to the hotel, and so Hutoc was now telling Christina the history of this area. He continued his story, telling us about the Nazi massacre at Lidice. He spoke mostly in English, but frequently crossed into German. Not understanding German, I had to wait for Christina's translations. Hutoc said many Czechs had supported Tito against the Russians. He was himself interested in how Fidel Castro would fare with the Russians.

"The sun rises in the East and sets in the West," he said. "But the coal rises in the West and sets in the East. Now maybe sugar too."

Back at the hotel, Art said that Hutoc had also talked about Che Guevara.

"Christina didn't translate that," I said. "What did he say about Guevara?"

"That Guevara was in Czechoslovakia recently. And that the Russians were angry about Guevara's Zurich speech."

First Paul Bertrand in Paris, now Mr. Jan Hutoc in Carlovivari. I lay in bed, thinking about these meetings. Had Christina really met Hutoc by chance? I remembered the bizarre stories she'd told me in San Francisco. On the plane to Paris, and in Paris, she'd been flirting with me. Why? She spoke fluent French, German, Spanish and English. What other languages did she speak? With all these skills, what was she doing in the People's Revolutionary Party, a tiny organization of no consequence? I thought about the FBI agents who had tried to recruit me as an informant. I'd refused, but that didn't mean others had. And if the FBI or CIA had spies in our group, perhaps other governments did also. But which of them was connected to Felicia's death?

In the morning I got Art to go back with me to the tavern where we'd met Christina and "Mr. Hutoc." Art asked the waiter, in fluent German, if he remembered us from the previous night. The waiter nodded. Art then asked about the man we had been talking to. The waiter stepped away from our table, stared at us, then walked away.

"What the hell!" I said.

"This is a different world," Sparrow said.

Before we got up to leave, a man who had been sitting alone at the back of the tavern stopped as he walked past. He tipped his hat, smiled at us, and said in perfect English, "Such a nice day, don't you think?"

Art and I just looked at each other.

11

The Cubana Airlines plane which took us from Prague to Havana was propeller driven and carried no other passengers but the thirteen in our group. When we stopped for refueling in Shannon, Ireland, the first argument broke out. Richard Thornton, the ex-preacher, accused Steve Bloomberg of flirting with Arlene Washington. Bloomberg tried to explain that he was only trying to be sociable. In fact, he'd been trying to recruit Arlene, and Thornton knew this. After refueling, we continued chugging slowly across the Atlantic Ocean.

I now learned that most of the group was from the coasts. The exceptions were Frank Vara, who claimed to be Chilean, and Thornton and Arlene Washington, who had both been raised in the South.

"Che Guevara and Fidel represent something the Communist world hasn't seen in decades," Monica Chapman told me. This tall, lanky, blonde girl who had known Felicia in the Fair Play Committee and with whom I'd driven across the country was full of surprises. She referred to herself humorously as a "palomino," but she had a backpack full of books about Latin America—which she was willing to loan—and was not only well-read but extremely smart and insightful. "I mean real debate about fundamental issues," she continued. "How do you go from capitalism to communism? By continuing to pit man against man, through competition, which is the capitalist way? This is what Che means when he talks about adhering to the law of value. Or do you immediately start to develop socialist man—moral, cooperative people who place the good of society above self-interest? Should profitability be given precedence over central planning? Should the economy be diversified, or should exports like sugar be emphasized? How much autonomy should individual factories have?"

I was impressed. Until then I'd been unaware of such issues. Monica said she intended to raise them with any Cuban leaders we met.

Richard Thornton, on the other hand, couldn't have cared less about socialist theory. He thought humanity—at least white humanity—was worthless and not capable of being improved.

"America is producing worse and worse human beings," he told me. "White Americans are capable, like the Nazis, of committing inhuman atrocities. That's what we're seeing in the South. Black people have always known this about whites."

Playing devil's advocate, I argued that human nature now was no better or worse than it had ever been.

"That's what they want you to think," Thornton's girlfriend, Arlene Washington, said.

"Who are *they*?"

"*They* are the people who want us to accept the status quo. *They* are the ruling class."

This attractive black woman seemed filled with anger. I asked her why that was, and she told the following story.

Arlene was from Mississippi and had migrated to the West Coast after her mother died. When she was a child, her father had been arrested for the rape and murder of a ten-year-old white girl. This man had farmed his own land and had never been in trouble. But when questioned by the police, he'd told them a story about trying to help the girl. When he saw she was dead, he'd gotten scared and run away. The trial went quickly. Arlene's father was sent to death row. When the day of the execution arrived, Arlene's mother had gone to the prison to witness it. She said that her husband's last words were not to feel sorry for him, that he was only one of many who would be crucified in this world but would find justice in the next.

"I don't know if he really said that or not," Arlene told Thornton and me. "It sounds more like something Mama would say. But the last thing she saw of my daddy in this life was the trap door opening and him falling through. That was when the bottom dropped out of our own lives. There was church, of course. But Mama got old before her time. Her main company was the dogs, which were old and gray like her. A few years after my daddy was put to death, the real murderer confessed. He was an insane man who was in jail for other crimes. Mama asked the governor for a pardon, but that never happened because it could've meant a lawsuit against the state of Mississippi. After that, Mama never talked about my daddy. I'd watch her climb into the same old bed she'd shared with him. She only slept on one side of it. The dogs would be around the bed, like they was protecting her."

As Arlene told me this story, I remembered the beggar Jake Campbell had pointed out to me in New York, the black man with the sign saying "27 years in an Alabama prison for stealing a chicken." Right now, cops with clubs and dogs were attacking civil rights marches, churches were being bombed, and jails were crowded with black men. Welfare rolls were filled with black women and children.

Thornton said that racism had supposedly been outlawed in Cuba. He and Arlene wanted to see if that was true.

Art and I played a few games of chess. He was a good player, having read chess books and studied classic games, so I had to concentrate. I upset him by leaving the seat when it was his turn to move, coming back when he'd made his move, immediately making my next move, then walking the aisles again. What Art didn't know was that I mentally "photographed" the chess board so that I could think about the game as I walked around.

At one point I sat next to Christina and told her about the Czech waiter's response when Art Sparrow had asked about him about Jan Hutoc.

"Do you think Hutoc was a policeman of some sort?" I asked.

"People in these countries are suspicious of strangers," Christina said.

"Art said Hutoc was talking about Che Guevara being in Prague. What was that about?"

"I don't think your friend's German is very good. Hutoc didn't say that." Then Christina changed the subject and began going over the itinerary of the trip. We'd be in Havana for a week or two, travel across the country for about a week, then return to Havana for the July 26th celebration before heading home. Hopefully we'd get to meet some important Cuban officials, as well as ordinary workers, farmers, and of course students. "By the way, Jake says we're already making news. One of the New York papers had a headline, 'American Students Defect to Communist Cuba.' That's great."

"Why is that great?"

"It's great because for us any publicity is good publicity. We don't expect truthful coverage. The media are owned by the corporations." I wanted to ask her more about Jan Hutoc, but Christina launched into a speech about how the media had distorted Fidel's visit to the United Nations when he'd stayed at the Hotel Theresa in Harlem, how everything the American press ever wrote about the People's Revolutionary Party was slanderous, and how militants like Malcolm X were never given fair coverage. She ended by saying, "But you can help us get the truth about Cuba to the American people."

"The truth," I said. "By the way, what were all these meetings in Carlsbad about?"

Christina said there was a fight going on within the party, and she was trying to mediate it.

"It's between Steve Bloomberg and Jake," she said. "Steve thinks that Jake is making decisions unilaterally. He thinks Jake chose too many unreliable people to join the trip."

"Unreliable?"

"We have at least one known spy with us. Steve thinks we should never have taken him, and that at least we should have kicked him out before getting to Cuba."

"Who is it?"

"Frank Vara. He works with right-wing Cuban exiles and probably also for the government. Jake's reasoning is that at least we know this one and can keep an eye on him and alert the Cubans."

The other contentious issue amongst the PRP comrades was that there were a couple of Trotskyites in the group. Bloomberg wanted them kicked out.

"Who are they?"

"Monica Chapman."

"The palomino?"

"And maybe Art Sparrow. They both have Trotsky books and are very critical of the Soviet leadershp. Jake says they can't be trusted, but they're no real danger. Felicia Vasquez was a Trotskyite too, you know."

I hadn't known this. Actually I wasn't at all sure what the term meant, besides being a pejorative. I felt uncomfortable discussing Felicia with Christina Ward, so I changed the subject and asked about Anne Montrose leaving the trip.

"Sometimes people who come on the most militantly cave in the easiest," Christina said. "I never trusted her."

I sat next to Frank Vara and tried to talk to him, but he ignored me.

It was Monica, the palomino, who started the next fight. Jake Campbell was reading a book. Monica snatched it away and in a loud voice demanded to know why he was spreading stories about her. Campbell denied he'd said anything about her.

"You're not only a filthy gossip. You're a liar," she shouted. "But for the record, I want everyone here to know that I worked with the Fair Play for Cuba Committee, and I don't give a damn if they were Trotskyites or… or stalactites. They were a lot more democratic than your group, and they didn't go around slandering people. I haven't been going around telling people how you try to fuck any woman you can, Jake, like Felicia Vasquez or Anne Montrose, or how you tried to get into my pants until I told you to back off or I'd cut your goddamn balls off."

12

My first impression of Cuba as we flew over the island was one of colors—deep, rich browns and greens—which made me think of the pale and faded colors of the European landscape I had so recently seen. By the time we touched down, most of the women had fixed their make-up and hair and had straightened their clothes, and several of the men, including me, had cameras out and were snapping pictures before we'd even left the plane. A crowd of Cubans welcomed us as if we were important dignitaries. We were swarmed by kids from the Federation of University Students, several official-looking people, and by the Cuban police, who came aboard the plane before we could leave, asking for Clifton Specks and taking him away in handcuffs. An officer spoke to Jake Campbell and showed him a copy of a newspaper. I was near Campbell and read the headline: "Fugitive Escapes to Cuba." The newspaper was from Miami. Clifton Specks's picture was below the caption. The article said that the FBI wanted Specks for the murder of a woman in San Francisco named Felicia Vasquez. I had to wait for Campbell to finish reading the front page and turn to the inside. Specks, the article continued, had a record of child molestation, and had spent several years in prison. The article stated further that the Committee to Uphold the Right to Travel, a front group of the People's Revolutionary Party, had helped Specks flee to Cuba in order to escape arrest.

I'd driven all the way across America with Felicia's killer, and had let him slip though my hands.

"They could've arrested him in New York before we left," Campbell said to no one in particular. He was angry. This story upstaged the story he wanted to see. "They let the bastard get on the plane just so they could smear us." Then he looked up and addressed the entire group.

"Don't let this incident engineered by the FBI and the State Department distract you. The real news is that we've just broken the travel ban. Now let's go and meet our hosts and begin our historic visit!"

Flashes popping and news cameras turning, twelve Americans, smiling and waving, now descended to the tarmac and were greeted by cheers. As the first of us to reach Cuban soil, Campbell delivered a short speech while everyone else waited behind him. I seethed, wondering if the Cubans would let me get close to Clifton Specks.

All around me, people shook hands and introduced themselves. Campbell and his comrades gave prepared statements to the Cuban media. But I stood in the hot sun of the Jose Marti airport and watched as four soldiers took Clifton Specks and disappeared into a building. The newspaper article had said that Specks was recently released from a prison mental hospital in New York where he'd served a term of six years for molesting an eight-year-old girl. Six years, then they'd let him go free, and he'd killed Felicia. Had there been others? I remembered that he'd disappeared sometimes when we'd stopped to eat on our cross-country trip. I'd assumed he'd wanted to eat alone. Had he been looking for more victims? Although he was fat and dirty and looked pathetic, I'd driven three thousand miles with him and had no idea he could be capable of assaulting or killing anyone. Of all the people in the group, he'd been my least likely suspect. I could imagine Felicia feeling sorry for him, letting him into her house…

I was told that Specks would be flown to Madrid on the next available plane, then transferred to the custody of United States marshals. After speaking with army and police officers and explaining to them that I was an American reporter covering this "historic" trip, I was finally allowed to see Specks, who was being held in a tiny room. When I entered, he was crying. During the trip across the country, I'd noticed the muscles around his left eye occasionally twitching. Now his left eyelid was twitching non-stop. I sat a few feet away from him asked if the newspaper story was true.

Specks said he'd played doctor with a little girl, and as a consequence had spent six years in a mental hospital.

"They want to castrate me," he said. "But I never touched her."

I spoke softly, although rage was building inside me. Remembering Anne Montrose's shopping trip to replace missing clothes, I said, "Clifton, did you take anything from any of us on the trip across country?"

He stared at me.

"Clifton, did you hurt Felicia?"

He continued to stare at me. Then he smiled. It was a weird smile. I thought he was taunting me. Unable to restrain myself any longer, I lunged at him. I punched his face and I punched his head and I did not stop until the Cuban guards forcibly tore me away.

When we finally left the airport and got on the bus for our hotel, I was still in shock. I watched as BJ and others took pictures of the city, and absent-mindedly noted the sign boards, which I could come back to later and photograph.

"CUMPLIREMOS – ESTUDIO, TRABAJO, FUSIL," "VIVA LA REVOLUTION LATINOAMERICANA," "EL INTERNACIONALISMO PROLETARIO."

There were also huge posters of Camilo Cenfuegos and other martyrs of the Revolution.

Art Sparrow wondered aloud why it was necessary to mythologize people who were just flesh and blood human beings. I didn't much like this Cuban propaganda either. In fact, I wanted to go back to the airport and return to the States with Clifton Specks. With Felicia's murder solved, the tension I'd been feeling was dissipating, and I realized I wasn't all that interested in Cuba.

"The Revolution is five years old," Art said. "Full of hope and energy and illusions."

Although the American press was playing up Clifton Specks' "escape" to Cuba, our group did get some coverage. Being the first American citizens to openly defy the travel ban, our names and pictures, as well as our home addresses, appeared in several articles. Anyone who might want to harass us or our families would know exactly where to begin.

Our hotel, the Havana Riviera, had been built by American gangsters before the Revolution, when Cuba had been wide open for gambling, prostitution, drugs, and whatever else tourists couldn't get at home. The hotel was a twenty-story curved structure near the beach, and had a huge swimming pool, a restaurant, a bar, a nightclub—which we were immediately told could be used for meetings—and several big rooms originally intended for gambling, now also used for meetings. Outside the hotel, on the plaza, a group of musicians from Guyana played steel drums and an armed militia stood guard.

The elevators worked, which apparently wasn't always the case in Cuban hotels, as did the air conditioning. The other guests were mostly Russians and East European technicians. Tourists from Western Europe, Asia, and Latin America stayed at other hotels. We were given rooms on the 18th floor, two people to a room. Each contained twin beds, a closet, a bathroom, and a small balcony. However, Jake Campbell and I were each assigned larger suites. These included a living room, and I was also provided with a typewriter and materials to develop film—black bags, boxes, and developer—so that I could set up a lab in my bathroom. From my balcony I had a view of the hotel swimming pool, the boulevard called "The Malecon," which stretched along the seafront, and the Florida Straits. After putting my things away, I fell asleep.

I slept through the rest of the day and most of the night and awoke in the early hours of the morning. After showering, I went down to the lobby and got a cup of coffee from the tourist office, which was the only office in the hotel open then. Two militiamen guarded the entrance. They told me the hotel staff took turns standing guard because there had been terrorist attacks at various facilities around the island. I sat on the hotel plaza with them and drank my coffee and thought about my situation. Since I was here for the several weeks, I decided I might as well make the best of it, take photographs and do some reporting. I was sure Felicia would have wanted me to see as much of Cuba as possible. From a guy in the tourist office, I got a copy of the itinerary the Cubans had planned for us. It was set to begin at ten that morning. I also got directions to the Prensa Latina office and set out immediately to see a bit of Havana.

It was already warm, so I stayed on the shady side of the Paseo, passing colonial-style buildings and houses painted bright colors. Whenever I stopped to take a picture, I wrote in my notebook a corresponding number so that later I could identify the photo. No one seemed to be following me. The streets were coming to life—buses, bicycles, old cars, people going to work. At the Plaza of the Revolution, I took pictures of the monuments, buildings, and banners. A few blocks farther on I was besieged by kids selling cigarettes, tickets to a cock fight, and access to beautiful girls. I picked up a Cuban newspaper. Our group's picture was on the front page, but Clifton Specks' arrest was not mentioned. At the Prensa office I introduced myself to Jose Zambala, who was anxious to help me with whatever I needed, including a desk in his office. I said I didn't need office space, but that I might need help developing photos. I asked Zambala for any wire service stories about Specks. The Associated Press story was the most extensive. Clifton had signed up to go on an illegal trip to Cuba that Felicia Vasquez had been planning. He had dated her several times before killing her, and he had worked for a Berkeley newspaper called the *Free Express*.

I asked Jose to use his phone and called my boss in Berkeley, where it was still very early morning.

"Other than the fact that they got you and him confused," Mrs. Wilson said, "they have no case against him. For one thing, as part of his release, he agreed to be castrated, and that procedure was completed. And he's been supervised by a parole officer who says Clifton wasn't even in California when Felicia was killed. I'd say it's unlikely the guy has the necessary sex drive. Or any other kind of drive."

13

So Jake Campbell was probably right. The government had used Clifton Specks to discredit the Committee. Probably he shouldn't even have been given a passport. So instead of students fighting to see the Cuban Revolution for themselves, the Committee to Uphold the Right to Travel was "helping a dangerous criminal escape justice." On the way back to the hotel I thought about my attack on Clifton, and I felt terrible. But if he was innocent, then Felicia's killers were still at large. Hoping it might give me an advantage, I decided to keep my mouth shut about what I'd learned from Mrs. Wilson. I was in Cuba to report on the Cuban Revolution and our group's tour.

Since the Cuban media were also covering our tour, every day we could also see ourselves on TV and in the newspapers.

Our official bus tour was grueling. Bus rides, heat, schools, uniformed children singing revolutionary songs—then more bus rides, heat, meetings with dignitaries who looked alike and spoke the same lines and ducked any real questions. Then more bus rides, heat, factories, more factories, vanguard workers with set speeches, more kids singing revolutionary songs, and, outside Havana, cooperative farms and state farms, vanguard farmers and vanguard managers. I only half-listened to the speeches, and if we'd been taken to the same factory over and over—how many could there be in an underdeveloped country?—I don't think any of us would have been the wiser. I wondered if the people who spoke to us at the University of Havana were the same people who had run the university under the old regime. Factory and farm managers recited statistics I had no way of checking and spoke endlessly of the progress and happiness the Revolution had bestowed. To get a feel for the country, I'd have to break away from the official tour and meet ordinary people.

Back at the hotel every afternoon, I developed film, wrote articles, and then delivered them to the Prensa Latina office, where they were wired or sent by mail to Mexico City.

The temperature climbed to a hundred, a hundred and five. Once in the morning and once in the middle of the afternoon, the sky would cloud over, and there would be a downpour lasting five or ten minutes. Then, for a while, you could breathe. But the heat would come again, as oppressive as before. Steam rose from the pavement. As soon as we returned to the hotel after one of our tours, people would run for their swim suits and head to the pool. At night a breeze, warm and pleasant and full of music and laughter, might sweep across the city.

After dinner the group would split up and we'd go out on the town. And late at night the drinking and partying would begin on the eighteenth floor. I wondered what the Cubans thought about these tiny but regular eruptions of bourgeois decadence in the middle of their well-planned Socialist tour. But from my balcony I could hear the splashes and laughter and shrieks of Americans. If I went down to the lobby, I might catch glimpses of one or another of the group leaving or entering someone else's room, and I'd usually see Art Sparrow in the lobby playing chess. There was an endless tournament at the hotel.

Havana itself was a city of contrasts—colonial churches, vintage American cars, tree-lined boulevards, modern hotels and skyscrapers, ancient buildings on the verge of collapse, monuments and banners with slogans, tiny fishing boats in the harbor alongside Soviet freighters. I was especially drawn to Old Havana, and I went there most nights. The movie theaters were cheap and played a lot of old Chaplin movies unavailable in the States. As I walked through the dark streets, alone or with Monica or Art, I wondered if we were being followed. Once, alone, I ducked into a doorway and waited. The footsteps I'd heard behind me stopped. When I started walking again, whoever was behind me stayed out of sight.

Mrs. Wilson was calling my series of stories "Travels with Che and Fidel," and thanks to the press services, the articles were being picked up by other newspapers. This made me something of a celebrity, and consequently made it a bit easier to talk to some of the people in the group. I divided our group into categories. First were members of the People's Revolutionary Party. They were either followers (Sharon Albright and Helen Anderson) or leaders (Jake Campbell, Steve Bloomberg, and Christina Ward). Campbell himself wanted to control the group's every move, as if he was afraid that if he let people wander off by themselves, something bad would happen. He liked to place himself so that he would be looking down at the person he was talking to. He would speak in tones which said, 'I know what I'm saying is too difficult for you to comprehend, so just take my word for things.' I wondered if Campbell practiced his facial expressions in front of a mirror. His rival, Steve Bloomberg, with his rolled up shirt sleeves, work pants, and wire-rimmed glasses, was always ready with a lecture about Marxism. When he made a point, he'd lean close and look a person in the eyes. His voice at such times was like a crowing cock's. Christina Ward acted as a liason between ourselves and our Cuban guides; she kept her distance from the rest of us. And the two followers—Sharon Albright and Helen Anderson—deliberately stayed in the background. Could Campell or Steve Bloomberg have drowned Felicia? After Christina's meetings in Paris and Carlsbad, I wondered if she could have been involved.

My next category included BJ Johnson, Richard Thornton, and Arlene Washinton, who, although they agreed with Campbell, weren't members—at least not yet—of the People's Revolutionary Party.

Then there were the people who were sympathetic to the Cuban Revolution but distanced themselves from Campbell. I assumed these people were on the trip because, although the PRP didn't hope to recruit them, the party planned to use them in some other way. They included Monica Chapman, the 'palomino' who had worked with Felicia in the Fair Play Committee; Frank Vara, whom I'd seen with gusanos in San Francisco; Art Sparrow, the lawyer; and of course myself.

With Clifton Specks back in the United States and Anne Montrose and others having opted out in New York, there were now twelve of us. At meals we sat four to a table in the hotel dining room. But our tables were so close that conversations could be carried on between them. These were mostly political arguments, ranging from the possibility of extending the Cuban Revolution to the rest of Latin America to the old

Stalin-Trotsky controversy about constructing socialism in one country. Although I was only mildly interested in these debates, I followed the conversations closely, on the lookout for a slip of the tongue or some other clue which might reveal a murderer. Several of the group had read Che Guevara's book, and one night BJ and Vara were arguing about the possibility of guerrilla warfare in the United States.

"It's basically a Maoist strategy," BJ said.

"And it worked for the Chinese," Vara said. So far I hadn't noticed the Cubans paying special attention to Vara. I wondered if Campbell had told them of our suspicion that Vara was a gusano.

"Yes, but they rode to power on a wave of peasant revolt, and the Kuomintang was so discredited and isolated—"

"It worked in Cuba too, didn't it?"

"Another country with a small urban proletariat," Monica Chapman said from her table. The tall blonde had first aroused the hostility of the PRP faction by publicly challenging Jake Campbell on the airplane. Now in Cuba—and to the dismay of the PRP—she'd become a favorite camera study for Cuban photographers.

"I'd say the Cubans were more influenced by what happened in Guatemala," BJ said.

While this argument was going on, Helen Anderson and Sharon Albright were discussing Cuban males, at my table. Helen, attractive but overweight, was telling Sharon Albright about our Cuban guide, Ricardo.

"Cuban men are all flirts," Helen said. "I thought they'd be more serious. Some nights this hotel is like a rabbit hutch."

"Ricardo—like on the Lucy show?" Sharon said.

"I think that Monica has a different man in her room every night. What must the Cubans think of us?"

"Why should they care?"

"They know everything we do. Somebody goes through my bureau every time I go out."

Richard Thornton and his girlfriend, Arlene, had also complained a few times about room searches. But tonight they were complaining about something else.

"They put too much sugar in everything," Thornton said loudly. Only thirty years old, Thornton already had the paunch of a middle-aged man.

"They grow the sugar here," Arlene said. "It's one thing they got plenty of."

"The question is this," Monica said. "Would guerrilla warfare work in a country like Argentina, with its industries and huge urban population?"

I wasn't the only one trying to listen to all the conversations. If Steve Bloomberg had leaned over any further, his chair would have toppled.

"He'll be on the bus with us," Helen said. Then I caught the name "Billy" and saw Sharon looking over at BJ, who was now talking to our other Cuban guide, Maria Montalvo. Although the guides ate with us, I noticed they didn't eat very much and never drank beer.

At the third table, Art Sparrow began lecturing Monica and BJ about the "transformation of the sociopolitical nature of the citizen," and the "individual versus the collectivity," whatever these things meant. At this point Christina Ward came to sit by me. We'd hardly spoken since arriving.

"You look so serious, Dante. What are you thinking about?"

"What's on the agenda for tomorrow?"

"First, we visit the University of Havana, where we'll meet with our official hosts. Then we'll visit the new art school. After lunch we're scheduled to meet President Dorticos."

"What about Fidel or Che?"

"We're supposed to meet them, but I'm not sure when. Fidel's known for just showing up spontaneously. Possibly this is because there have been several attempts on his life. Anyway, you should be prepared."

"I've always got a camera with me."

"I've been meaning to ask you, but we've just been so busy. Do you really think Clifton murdered Felicia?"

The question took me by surprise. At the next table, Art and Monica were arguing. The 'palomino' said, "The U.S. will not let it happen again, believe me. Latin America is too vital to American interests." Then Art said, "We didn't really understand how serious Fidel was, did we?" And from another table, Thornton called out, "They call this meat? I call it horse flesh. It's like their beer, which tastes like piss." Arlene Washington said, "The Coke tastes real."

"Have you heard anything about him?" Christina asked.

I lied and shook my head.

"I've got to meet with Jake for a few minutes. There's a bar a few blocks from the hotel that plays American jazz."

I said I'd already discovered the place.

"Would you meet me there for a drink in about an hour?"

I nodded and watched her go to a table at the side of the room and sit with Campbell and our Cuban guides. I'd noticed that whenever the guides had a question, they'd go to Christina, not to Campbell, for an answer.

Steve Bloomberg was telling Art that in Cuba a beard, which Art was now growing, signified that one had been a guerrilla fighter, and that Sparrow should shave his beard since he hadn't earned the right to wear it. At the table to my right someone said, "Have you read Fidel's speeches?" Someone else said, "Santeria? Never heard of it." A third voice: "This witch or priestess can tell things that are happening hundreds of miles away." And to my left someone said, "Stalin was a butcher. So is Mao."

What was Christina up to? I couldn't figure her out. She was shaking her head. One of the Cuban guides, Ricardo, was writing something down. "Man, that's what the U.S. government wants you to believe." From another direction: "It's a fundamental question."

What was a fundamental question?

Somebody was talking about the irrationality of individual greed. Art Sparrow was making a play for Monica.

Christina and Campbell got up. Watching her as she moved towards the door, I felt guilty. What were Sparrow and Monica talking about? I didn't know anything. Least of all did I know Christina Ward. She met people in different countries and conversed with them in their own languages. Now she wanted to have a drink with me.

Somebody said, "We use the workers' anger to turn things around, and by making the oppressed into the oppressor, we will achieve a just and rational society, no longer national but international, no longer class-based but classless."

Thornton said, "And if you can believe that, I've got a few bridges to sell you."

"You're an asshole." This was Bloomberg.

I was still staring at Christina and Campbell, who had both paused in the doorway. Then they left.

"A benevolent dictator, but still a dictator," Art said. "If tomorrow he decides to eliminate all midgets, we'll see posters all over Havana telling us midgets are imperialist lackeys, and the whole population will be chanting slogans to that effect."

People were drifting away from the tables, getting ready to party or go out on the town. Helen and Sharon were still at my table. BJ was alone at his.

"All the guys are fascinated by Cuban women," Helen whispered. She was looking at Maria Montalvo, our lovely guide, who was coming our way. Looking at her, I felt another pang of guilt. I missed Felicia, and Christina had me confused.

"But we have Cuban men," Sharon whispered.

14

The bar where I was supposed to meet Christina was a hangout for some of the American exile community. Most of them were middle-aged or older and had jobs with the Cuban government. Waiting for Christina to show up, I talked to a guy named Milt, who had been a member of the American Communist Party and who had been blacklisted during the McCarthy Period. On the other side of me sat a younger man, Robert Williams, who called himself "a political exile." He was facing criminal charges in North Carolina for what he called "exercising the right of self-determination." Both men had nothing but praise for Cuba's accomplishments.

When Christina showed up, we moved to a table in back.

"I just thought we should touch base," she said. "I've been so busy. We haven't really seen much of each other since since the flight over."

I started right in. "Your French friend, the guy you talked to in Paris—"

"Bertrand? Yes, he's the editor of a socialist magazine in Paris."

"And Jan Hutoc, the guy in Carlsbad?"

"What are you trying to say?"

"There were plenty of people, reporters with much more experience you could've gotten to come on this trip. Why did you invite me?"

"Because I trust you."

"That story you told me in San Francisco, about you and your father traveling from country to country—was any of it true?"

"It was all true. But I didn't tell you everything about myself. Would you like me to?"

"Yes. What's the rest?"

"My real name is Sanchez. Ward was my ex-husband's name. My father was a teacher, and we did travel a lot." Christina reached over and placed her hand on mine. "Can we go back to the hotel and talk there? I don't like this place, all these expatriates."

On the way back to the hotel Christina took my arm. Then, suddenly, she stopped in the middle of the dark street and turned as if to ask me a question. Instead she kissed me. It was a short kiss. She waited for me to return it, but I didn't. We didn't talk the rest of the way, although she still held onto my arm.

Back at the hotel, a party was in full swing. Guests milled about the swimming pool and the lobby. Somebody had brought musicians, and Dick Thornton was playing bongo drums with them. A few Soviet technicians and some Cubans had joined in. As Christina and I walked through the lobby, BJ and Sharon tried to hand us drinks, but we made our way to the elevator and went up to my room.

"Dave Swan," Christina said. We were sitting out on the balcony.

"Who?"

"That's who I thought of when I heard about Felicia. But of course he was dead."

"Who is—was—Dave Swan?"

"A nut. Half the members of the party are nuts. The other half are FBI. Sometimes you can't tell the difference. The clever nuts say they're agents, and the clever agents pretend they're nuts."

I didn't know what she was talking about. I asked her again about this person Dave Swan, but she ignored my question and asked her own.

"Have you been followed?"

"I'm not sure."

"Of course, it's to be expected. What was that?"

"What was what?"

"I heard it before, and there it is again."

We sat in silence for a few minutes.

"That click—I heard it when we first came in," Christina said.

I hadn't heard anything.

"There's a click. It comes about every ten minutes. Wait."

We sat in silence. I still didn't hear anything.

"It's going to happen any second. Listen."

I listened. Then I heard it, and I knew exactly what it was. I got up. One of my cameras—the one with the timer, which I would set up in front of a dignitary at an interview so as to allow me to wander around with a smaller camera—had been placed on the mantle and turned on. I turned it off. It had been set for ten minutes. I took the camera into the bathroom and closed the door. This camera should have been empty. But about half of one of my largest rolls of film had been shot—shots of the empty room, mostly underexposed shots which the camera had taken when the lights were out. I made a contact print and brought it out. Christina had come in from the balcony. Sounds of music drifted up from streets. Out on the Florida Strait I could see the lights of a ship.

"Somebody's been playing with my camera."
"You didn't set this up?"
"Why would I?"
"I don't know. You tell me."
"I guess it's somebody's idea of a joke. It's the sort of prank my old roommate would pull."
"I have to go," Christina said. And I watched as she brushed past me and went out the door.

Over the next couple of days I saw Christina only in passing. Partly this was because I was skipping the official tour and wandering around by myself. But she was definitely avoiding me. She'd smile when we passed at the hotel, then keep going. I wondered if she was sleeping with someone. I visited Monica Chapman in her room and asked her to fill me in on the latest gossip. Dick Thornton, she said, was making regular trips to an area of the Malecon where the prostitutes plied their trade. Thornton couldn't keep his hands to himself, but his girlfriend, Arlene, ignored or accepted his wanderings. Frank Vara was considered handsome by Sharon Albright, and Steve Bloomberg was trying to get into Christina Ward's bed, but had so far been unsuccessful. Helen Anderson was in love with BJ, but BJ, although friendly, didn't share the passion. And Campbell was trying to seduce Maria Montalvo, our Cuban guide.

I was in the lobby one night, watching the chess games and listening to the steel drum band, when Dick Thornton approached and asked if I wanted to play a game. But Thornton wasn't really interested in chess. After a few moves he began complaining that Campbell was autocratic and wasn't listening to the rest of us.

I nodded.

Then Thornton said that James Baldwin's book *Go Tell It on the Mountain* had made him leave the church in order to pay more attention to the problems of black folk.

I nodded again.

"I read the story you wrote a while back about the march we had for the little girls who were bombed in the church. I was one of the main speakers at that march, but you didn't even mention me. You had a picture of some fool who didn't have anything to do with it."

I nodded.

He leaned across the chess board and whispered, "I have a proposition for you."

Thornton's proposition was that I should do a special interview with him, an exclusive story about a black American's reactions to Cuba.

I said I'd think about it.

When I got back upstairs and turned down the hallway to my room, I found Helen Anderson with her ear pressed to my door. I backed up so that I wouldn't be seen. When I peeked again, the door to my room was closing. I waited a minute, then went to my room and opened the door. Helen's back was to me. She was going through a story I'd just written. I closed the door.

"What are you doing?"

Helen dropped the pages onto the coffee table and came towards me. "I was just looking," she said.

"Why?"

"We want to know what you're writing."

"You've been in here before, haven't you?"

Helen didn't answer.

"Are you sneaking into all the rooms, or am I special?"

"I don't have to answer your questions. Let me by."

I'd already suspected that since not all my articles about Cuba had been positive, somebody had been looking through my notes. My first negative article had been in response to declarations of support for the Cuban Revolution, statements made by various members of the group at a meeting of the Mothers of Martyrs of the Revolution. Steve Bloomberg had made a speech and had received great applause. Then Thornton made a speech, in English, which I thought was mainly to get attention. But it was all-American BJ Johnson who had rubbed me the wrong way. He'd brought the Cubans to their feet by proclaiming that the youth of the United States supported them. Johnson's speech was broadcast on Cuban television, and he was identified as the student body president of one of the largest universities in the United States. In my article, I'd pointed out that Johnson represented no one but himself.

I looked through the typed copy Helen had been going through. It was not the stories of the group's visits to factories and schools, but rather my articles about everyday Cubans. It had turned out that average people were quite willing to talk to me. The first pages were about Julio, a man I'd asked for directions and who then invited me into his home. Forty years old, originally from Santa Clara, he'd been a farmer and now worked in construction. His wife, Luisa, was learning to type. Their apartment was small but clean.

I read what Julio had told me. "Since the Revolution, our rent is ten percent of our wages. And there is always food on the table and milk for the children." This was enough to make him and his wife supporters of the Revolution, and it made for a nice article. The next story was about a waiter who told me that because the owners had left for Miami, the employees now ran the restaurant as a cooperative. Then there were pages about fishermen, teachers, students, and random people I'd stopped on the streets. Most of them said the Revolution was bettering their lives. Of course, cars and buildings needed repairs, and clothing was in short supply. I'd written that many people had offered to buy the clothes off my back. But they seemed healthy. Even the skeptics, like the guy in the boatyard, were proud of what their country was accomplishing.

"Before the Revolution," the black laborer had told me, "the beaches had ropes to keep us on one side. Now the ropes are gone."

"We are just a small country," a medical student had said. "The doctors—they served only the rich. And they left the country when the rich left. Now we have hospitals even in the mountains."

I played devil's advocate and said things like, "But Castro is a dictator."

No doubt Jake Campbell wouldn't like that. In these pages I also wrote about the Literacy Campaign which Felicia had participated in, and I pointed out that truly repressive regimes do not educate, or arm, their subjects. But there were several pages, enough for three or four articles at least, about people who didn't like Fidel or the Revolution, like the people who had been arrested during the Bay of Pigs invasion, or people who said they were spied on by their neighbors. In one article, I'd written about the Committees for the Defense of the Revolution. Supposedly justified by the continual sabotage, these committees seemed like massive spying operations, neighbor snitching on neighbor. But taxi drivers and people who had worked around the hotels that had catered to tourists before the Revolution had been the most vociferous with their criticisms. Of course, these were only individuals. They knew, and I knew, that if anyone tried to organize an opposition, they would be jailed.

My most critical articles were gone. I assumed Helen must have taken the ones about uniformed children marching and repeating slogans (which for me was the most disturbing thing) as well as the mass meetings we'd been taken to. The themes of those meetings were always the same—discipline, organization, cooperation. There were endless clenched-fist salutes, revolutionary slogans, and mass chants.

When I confronted Jake Campbell about Helen Anderson's thievery and asked for my articles back, Campbell naturally denied everything. I reminded him about his promise that I wouldn't be censored. Then I rewrote those articles and sent them to the *Free Express*.

Richard Thornton approached me with another proposition.

"Cuba is just one step," the preacher said. "Just one small country. What I want, for my people, you understand, is to visit all these Communist countries—China and Russia, East Germany, all of them. I don't want this tour to be just one month. I think it should be longer, so I can make a complete report to the black community at home. You get what I'm saying? And I need a reporter to come with me and Arlene."

I said I'd think about it.

Later that day, Thornton gave me an application he'd gotten from the Chinese Embassy for travel to China. The application had questions like,

"What is the class background of your parents?" I didn't think I wanted to visit China.

The Cubans, in spite of the criticisms which the People's Revolutionary Party apparently found distasteful, continued to make sure I had whatever I needed, especially film and developer. I was taking scores of photographs—children's faces, campesinos cutting sugar cane in the fields outside Havana, an illegal cock fight, taxi drivers in their old American cars, militia standing guard outside businesses, children in uniform and holding flowers and flags, Che Guevara's offices lit up at night high above the Plaza of the Revolution. I photographed slums and other signs of the poverty which five years of revolution had not yet overcome, and I went to a school for former prostitutes in what before the Revolution had been an exclusive neighborhood for the wealthy, but where now the mansions had been converted to student housing. I asked to visit the prisons, but was denied permission. And I asked repeatedly for interviews with Castro and Guevara.

I was sending in articles and photographs about Cuba every day, but so far I'd gotten nowhere with my private investigation into Felicia's death. That was about to change.

15

I was in my room working on an article about Alicia Alonzo, the dancer. About midnight I poured myself a rum and Coke and went out on the balcony. That was when Christina knocked. I was surprised. I started to ask her if she'd care for a drink, but she cut me off and said she needed to use the bathroom.

"It's a mess," I said. "I use it for a dark room."

I poured drinks and took them out to the balcony and waited. When Christina finally came out, she looked distracted. She said she was feeling a little sick and would take a raincheck on the drink. If she felt better, she'd come back later. She didn't.

The next morning we were scheduled to visit Pinar Del Rio, a valley on the western end of the island. At Vinales, we were taken into Cuba's famous limestone caverns and saw an underground river. In the darkness I caught up with Christina and asked if she was feeling better. She said she was fine. I tried to joke with her about a ghostly figure rowing a boat, taking us across the river Styx. That was when, just in front of us, Steve Bloomberg pushed Frank Vara into the water. Vara came out swinging. He knocked Bloomberg down, then confronted Jake Campbell and our guides, Ricardo Martinez and Maria Montalvo. Bloomberg, whose ego had been bruised worse than his jaw, shouted, "You're a goddamn gusano!"

The rest of the trip was uneventful. But by the time we got back to Havana, I felt exhausted. I went to my room, flopped on the bed, and fell asleep.

It was dark when I awoke. Somewhere outside, someone was screaming. I got up and went out on the balcony. Below me, the hotel pool was fully lit. A crowd milled about. Then I saw an ambulance. Automatically picking up a camera, I headed downstairs. When I got there, the ambulance was driving off. Several of our group were standing around. The closest person to me was Art Sparrow, and I asked him what was going on.

"It's Christina Ward," he said. "She drowned."

"What?"

"Christina Ward!" Monica Chapman screamed. "They found her in the pool!"

"She was drunk," Helen Anderson said.

I looked at the Havana Riviera swimming pool. It was a very large six-sided pool, the shallow end situated nearest to the lobby. There were several lanes for swimming laps. I'd seen Christina swim there effortlessly. She was a strong swimmer, in great shape. She drank occasionally, but I'd never seen her drunk. In fact, Campbell or somebody else had been drinking her rations of beer at lunch and dinner. Then how could she drown?

For the rest of the night, people told and retold the same story, which was that Christina had been partying and had then gone swimming.

The whole thing was crazy. How it was possible that this woman, who was always in control of herself, should suddenly get so drunk that she drowned? How was it possible for a strong swimmer, which she was, to drown? How it was possible, even if she'd been drunk, that she could drown in a pool which, except for the deepest third, an adult could stand up in?

"Are you okay?" Art Sparrow said, and put an arm around my shoulder.

"I don't believe this was an accident," I said. I couldn't stop staring at the pool.

"Accidents happen, Dante."

Art went with me up to my room. We both sat down with drinks.

"Christina and I went out for drinks a while back," I said. "She didn't even finish hers." Now I remembered that when we'd come back from the jazz club, somebody had set up one of my cameras, the one with the timer. After that it was as if she'd been afraid to come near me. I said, "She came here last night. She went to the bathroom then left abruptly."

I went out on the balcony. I must've been out there for a long time. When I came inside again, Art had left.

The next morning Jake Campbell called a meeting in the hotel dining room. This man, who usually enjoyed being a leader and talking, now seemed at a loss for words. For a moment I thought he was going to lead us in prayer. Instead he only repeated what everybody already knew.

"The Cuban government," he said, "will ask for special permission from the United States to fly her body to Florida tomorrow—or today, rather. What time is it? Father Martin, a Maryknoll priest who lives in Cuba, will accompany her... the body."

Steve Bloomberg got up and whispered to Campbell. We were all waiting for more, but Campbell walked away before anyone could ask questions. On his way out of the dining room, he paused in front of me and asked me to meet with him for a few minutes in his room.

"This is tragic," Campbell said. He was sitting on the edge of the bed in his room. He gestured for me to sit in a chair. "Christina was a fine person. I didn't sleep all night. One of the hotel people saw her floating in the pool. Then the ambulance came. I can't believe this. What they told me is that she was drunk and that she'd taken off her clothes to swim." Campbell rubbed his face. "Of course, beyond the personal tragedy for her and her family, this is the worst thing that could happen. The American press will jump all over it. Castro has been informed. The Cubans will do everything to cooperate. Father Martin is going to accompany the body. Jesus, I can't believe this." He looked up at me. "Dante, what I wanted to tell you is that there's a lot riding on how this is covered in the press. I'm not trying to tell you what to write. The Cubans won't try to tell you what to write. But surely you can see how delicate the situation is. After the Missile Crisis, and right-wingers trying to blame Cuba for the Kennedy assassination, now this? My God!"

"I'd like to talk to the medical examiner," I said. "I also want to talk to the person who found her in the pool."

"Of course."

"If what I write is going to have any credibility, I need to speak to everybody involved."

Campbell nodded.

I went to Christina's room. Monica Chapman was there, packing Christina's things to be shipped back to the States.

"This stinks," I said.

Monica looked up at me.

"Christina was a good swimmer, and she didn't drink," I said.

"You didn't see her drink. That doesn't mean she never drank."

"Did you ever see her drink?"

"I went to bed early," Monica said. "I was tired after the trip yesterday. I'm so sorry for any mean things I ever said about her."

I hadn't heard these things, but I let Monica's comment go for now. "So who saw her drinking?" I asked.

"What are you trying to say?" She looked at me. "Let's not get paranoid, Mr. Reporter."

"This stinks," I said again.

"She couldn't handle her booze. That's all there is to it. Don't try to blow it up."

I took a cab to the hospital where the body had been brought. But I was told it was already on its way to the United States. I asked to speak with the coroner or whoever had done the autopsy, but I was told this wouldn't be possible. Some official said that at the request of "the girl's father," the autopsy would be performed in the United States.

I got back to the hotel about noon. The hotel staff who had discovered the body could not be located for me to interview—nor could the police officers or medics who had been called to the hotel. So I decided to write a story with the one fact I had—that Christina Ward was dead—plus my own questions and suspicions, and to hell with Jacob Campbell and all these Cubans who were so damn cooperative that I still hadn't learned a thing. On the way to my room I noticed that the pool was still operating. Since the day's official tour had been cancelled, several members of our group were out there swimming or sunbathing.

"They haven't changed the water yet," I said to Thornton, who passed me in the lobby in his swimming suit.

In my story I emphasized the lack of cooperation I was getting from the Cubans, my doubts about Christina being drunk, and my personal knowledge that she'd been a good swimmer. I also described the pool. I decided to have my photographs wired from the Prensa office, along with some shots I had of Christina. Because the quality wouldn't be good, I would also send developed photos by plane to Mexico City. When I got back to the hotel, Jake Campbell was waiting for me in the lobby.

"You can't write this," he said. He was holding a copy of the article I thought I had just sent off. He stepped close to me, toe to toe. "Are you trying to turn this into an international incident?"

"I've been trying all day to get information," I said as calmly as I could. We were standing in the middle of the lobby. "The Cubans are stonewalling me. Or they're lying. And you're standing too close, Jake. Your breath stinks."

Campbell stepped back. He changed his pose. "Will you at least wait a few hours before sending this off?"

"We had an understanding. No censorship. First I find Helen Anderson in my room reading my notes, and now you've got—"

"You don't have the facts."

"I'm trying to get them."

"Can you wait and talk to Sharon? She's hysterical. She went for a walk with Helen. As soon as they get back to the hotel, I'll bring her to your room."

An hour later, Sharon, Helen, and Jake Campbell came to my room. Sharon was a pretty girl but, I thought, a bit stupid. I hadn't had much to do with her. In New York I'd seen her answering telephones and typing in the Lower East Side offices of the People's Revolutionary Party. Now, as she virtually collapsed and sat on the floor, her eyes were red and puffy. Campbell asked her to tell me what she'd told him. After a long pause and without looking up, she began her story.

"We were partying," Sharon said. "Christina, Steve, Helen, some Cubans and me. We were drinking and—" she glanced up at Campbell— "well, some weed. I don't know who got it or where they got it. Here though, I think, in Havana." She turned to me. "Dick Thornton gave it to me. I don't think Christina was used to smoking because she coughed, you know, like it was her first time. After that she started drinking too. Can I have some water, please?" Helen brought her a Coke I'd been planning to use to make myself a drink. Sharon drank from the bottle. Some of the Coke spilled down her chin.

"We were all staggering around, looking for one of those street parties you see at night. But we didn't find any. We went to a bar. Then we came back to the hotel. Steve was hitting on Christina and me, sort of cute but also obnoxious." She took another swig of Coke and spilled more down her chin but didn't wipe it. "We decided to go for a swim. I don't know whose idea it was. Maybe it was mine. We all took off our clothes and got in the pool. Christina and I were the last ones to stay. I was just so out of it. When I got out, she said something like 'Don't leave me,' but I had to get to my room before I passed out."

Sharon stopped and lowered her head so that her hair fell over her face. Her shoulders started to shake.

"I should've stayed. We were all so drunk... But I didn't. I couldn't... I got out and I left her there... I went to my room, I don't know how I made it, and the next thing..."

After Helen took Sharon back to their room, Campbell said, "She doesn't want this to come out. You can understand that. She feels awful. I don't see what's to be gained by making this public."

"Do you know a Frenchman named Bertrand?" I said.

"No. Why?"

"Doesn't your party have connections, official or unofficial, with a French Communist organization?"

"No, we do not."

"What about a French Communist magazine?"

"I don't know what you're talking about."

"What about Jan Hutoc," I said, "that guy you and Christina met in Czechoslovakia?"

"Aucielo, you're paranoid. That was some old guy who wanted to talk about the Resistance in World War Two."

"And he just approached you and Christina in a tavern there?"

"Christina and I were having dinner. He heard us speaking English, and introduced himself, and we invited him to have a drink."

Christina hadn't lied. Or maybe Campbell was lying now. I had no way of knowing. I said, "What can you tell me about her background—family, that sort of thing?"

"I met Christina at City College. In 1961, I think. I was speaking about socialism, and she approached me after the talk and took a leaflet. I invited her to our headquarters for a forum. I think it was Tom Kinkaid, the chairman of our party at the time, who was speaking that night. After a few more contacts and some long conversations, we recruited her."

"Who was Dave Swan?"

"Dave Swan? What's he have to do with this? The guy's dead."

"I'm just curious. Who was he?"

"Christina had a brief relationship with him. Maybe it wasn't even a relationship. He was mentally disturbed and committed suicide. Nobody can blame her for that. Maybe some people did, but it wasn't fair. She was beautiful, and he was obsessed with her."

"What do you know about her family?"

"I never met them. She told me she'd traveled a lot as a kid because her father was an executive for some company with branches in different countries. That's why she knew languages like Spanish and French."

"And German," I said.

"I don't know. Russian, German—I suppose."

"Do you think she might've had connections with, say, any Cuban exiles?"

"That's ridiculous. You're trying to make something sensational out of a tragic accident."

"Do you think Felicia Vasquez's death was also a tragic accident?"

"What's Felicia got to do with Christina Ward?"

"That's what I'm trying to find out."

I asked Art, who was sharing a room with Frank Vara, if he knew where Vara had been when the "accident" occurred. Art said that he and Vara had gone to Old Havana. Then they'd come back to the hotel and gone to bed. Their room was small, with twin beds, and Art said that as far as he knew Vara hadn't gone out again. I also asked if he knew about Thornton giving marijuana or any other drugs to Sharon Albright.

Art nodded. Weed was easy to get in this city. He'd seen Thornton getting stoned with Sharon a few times.

"He probably screwed her," Art said.

I found Frank Vara in the hotel lobby playing chess with Thornton. I waited for them to finish, and when it was over, I asked Vara to take a walk with me. We left the hotel and crossed the boulevard and walked along the Malecon.

"What's on your mind?" Vara said.

"I know you work with the Cuba Libre organization," I said, hoping it might loosen him up.

"I don't deny it, but it's not what you think. I hate those bastards."

"Then what is it?"

"I'm sorry. I'm not at liberty to tell you. But trust me. You think I know something about Christina Ward's accident, is that it?"

I waited.

"Let us—let the Cuban authorities deal with this." Vara smiled at me. "You asked me what I am. I'm your friend. And I was Felicia's friend."

"You lived near her on Precita—"

"Yes. In fact, I got her that apartment. And I was there many times." Looking straight into my eyes, Vara squeezed my arm, then turned and walked back to the hotel.

Christina was dead. I had no proof, but I knew she'd been murdered, like Felicia, and that her killer was somebody in our group. And now Frank Vara, who admitted knowing Cuban exiles and admitted having been to Felicia's apartment, was implying—what? That he was Cuban Intelligence? I looked around. On one side the sea, on the other Havana. There was no one else in sight. I was alone.

16

At dinner that night, everyone was discussing the drowning. I was sitting at a table with Thornton, Arlene, and BJ, not paying much attention to their conversation, when suddenly I realized that Thornton and Arlene were arguing about where Arlene had been the previous night.

"You were in his room," Thornton said. "I know that."

"You know that." Arlene raised her voice. "What else do you know?"

Our table was the center of attention, but neither Thornton nor Arlene seemed to care.

"You were cheating on me," he said.

"Like you been cheating on me?"

Thornton lowered his voice so that only those of us at his table could hear him. "I'd rather jack off than go to bed with you anyway. It's better."

Arlene stared down at her plate. BJ and I watched as she got up and left the dining room. Thornton continued eating.

Then BJ stood up and announced there would be a meeting. Anyone who wanted to discuss the accident was welcome to stay.

"We're all upset," BJ said. "So far there's been a lot of gossip, and confusion. I think we should hear from anyone who was actually with Christina last night."

No one objected, but no one got up to speak either. Sharon Albright sat silently at her table.

"Somebody must've seen something," BJ said. "Somebody must know what happened."

Still no one spoke up.

Finally Monica Chapman said, "I saw her at dinner, and she wasn't drunk. She never even drank her beer. Jake, you usually drank hers." There was a small chuckle from somewhere.

"Dick, you were talking to her after dinner," BJ said.

"So what? Why don't you ask him what happened?" Thornton pointed at Campbell.

"Nobody's accusing anybody of anything," BJ said. "We're just trying to understand what happened. Didn't anybody see her after dinner?"

"She was at that bar up the street, the jazz place," Helen Anderson said.

"She didn't drink, and everybody knows it," Monica said.

"I didn't say she was drinking," Helen shouted. "I just said she was there. With Sharon and me and some Cubans. And you, Steve."

"What was she doing at the pool in the middle of the night?" Art asked.

During the next few minutes several more people asked questions. I saw Campbell whispering to Sharon, and finally she walked over and stood next to BJ. Tearfully she now told the group the same story she'd told me earlier.

After the meeting, I went up to my room. I'd been there only a few minutes when there was a knock on the door. It was a Cuban in a military uniform. The man handed me some papers, documents concerning the examination of Christina Ward's body. This man had not himself been present at the examination of the body. But his documents said that a blood sample revealed that Christina had been drinking alcohol.

I still didn't see how even a non-swimmer, drunk or sober, could drown in that pool.

An hour later I was visited by a Cuban police detective and a medical examiner, Dr. Romez, who told me the same story. The functionaries all agreed—the night of her death, Christina Ward had been drinking.

The next morning we were informed at breakfast that we would be going to Varadero, a resort a few hours from Havana, for an overnight stay. Ricardo, our guide, told us that before the Revolution Cuba had been known as a tropical paradise, free of North American prudery and restrictive laws. Ernest Hemingway, he said, wasn't the only American to seek refuge here.

"Except for the occasional hurricane, like Flora last year, our island was advertised for its beaches, beautiful women, gambling casinos, sport fishing, and nightclubs. Our most famous resort was Varadero Beach, which is now a vacation resort for vanguard workers."

I wanted to stay in Havana and investigate Christina's death, but I was not given a choice. This trip was clearly intended to distract us from the "accident" and get us out of Havana.

The roads outside Havana were tortuous, especially in a bus with no air conditioning. Looking around, I wondered which of my traveling companions was the murderer. Was Thornton, complaining again about the heat, just the ex-preacher and politician he claimed? He was a big man. I could imagine him holding a small woman under water. Jake Campbell? Art Sparrow? BJ? Steve Bloomberg? Perhaps a woman—would a woman be strong enough? But what did a killer look like?

Varadero wasn't exactly a tour of the Cuban countryside. But if the exquisite beach, luxury hotel, and nightclub were not enough to distract us from Christina's death, Fidel himself showed up. He came in a convoy of jeeps along with about twenty soldiers. As soon as he pulled up to the hotel, people recognized his entourage, left what they were doing, and came running and smiling to talk to him or just to listen and watch. Dressed in army fatigues, the soldiers acted more like buddies on an excursion than bodyguards accompanying their nation's leader. Castro himself—immediately surrounded by people he seemed to know—asked about somebody's cattle and somebody else's crops and another person's job. Maria, our guide, said this was his normal routine, to show up somewhere and find out firsthand what people were thinking. He moved the crowd towards our group. As he greeted us, he noticed we were standing by a ping-pong table and asked if anyone would like to play a game.

The students were thrilled, and while people snapped photographs, various members of our group now took turns at the paddle. Fidel kept up a non-stop conversation as he played. And he was good. BJ, his first opponent, scored three points. Then Dick Thornton took the paddle and scored. Fidel paused, took off his shirt, and concentrated. He was sweating, talking, laughing—obviously enjoying himself. The soldiers and the crowd looked on, cheering as Fidel won seven straight points. Then Jake Campbell took the paddle and won two points. Then Bloomberg and Monica took turns, but couldn't score. Fidel was winning, 14 to 12. Helen Anderson tied up the game, but Arlene lost three points. It was 17 to 14. Art Sparrow lost two points, but BJ came back and won two points. It was now 19 to 16. Art made it 19 to 18. Fidel, telling us he had to get somewhere but that we would see him again, finished the game against Bloomberg and Campbell, beating "our team" 21 to 18.

It was as if Christina Ward had never existed.

Castro, still talking, put his shirt on. Maybe we'd see him again, maybe we wouldn't. But my questions couldn't wait.

"Commandante," I called out in Spanish. "The woman in our group who drowned in Havana—what are you doing to investigate this death?"

Castro was tucking in his shirt. He stopped and looked at me. Then he turned around and said something to a man with a white beard. When he turned back he very solemnly expressed his regrets and condolences.

"We are investigating, Señor, Aucielo" he said. "As you realize"—he was now walking towards me through the crowd—"relations between our two countries are difficult, and this is a sensitive situation." Looking around at the entire group, he said, "So I ask for your patience."

There was silence.

I'd gone this far, and I had nothing to lose. I said, "Mr. President, this is the second death of a young woman who was trying to help the Cuban Revolution. The first death occurred in the United States. The victim's name was Felicia Vasquez."

Castro shook his head and lifted his hands, palms up, as if to say that this was all news to him. He frowned and looked again at the man with the white beard, and they spoke a few words. When Castro turned back, he said, "Yes, we met with Senorita Vasquez during the Literacy Campaign. I assure you, Comrade Aucielo, we take terrorism seriously. As you know, we have been constantly attacked and are being attacked every day."

The man with the white beard whispered something in Fidel's ear.

Again there was silence. Castro turned to face us

"We'll meet again," he said. The ghost of a smile appeared on his face. "Perhaps I'll give you another chance to try to beat me at ping-pong."

Then he turned, and was gone.

I was ostracized by everyone except Monica and Art, who went swimming with me that afternoon. We waded out from the beach about a hundred yards, and, standing on a sandy bottom in a few feet of warm water, I told them about the problems I'd encountered trying to investigate Christina's death.

Sparrow, who had apparently thought Christina's death accidental, was silent. Monica cautioned me to be careful.

That night we were treated to an old-style evening at the Varadero nightclub, including a stage show, a bottle of champagne on each table—followed by rum—and a Latin band. I watched Thornton and BJ, who were both excellent dancers, dance with all of the women in our group, even our guide, Maria.

17

The next day we returned to Havana. I was still trying to decide what, if anything, I should write about Christina's death. After showering, I came down to the lobby and sat on a couch. The militia guards were playing chess, the clerk was reading a Lenin pamplet behind the main desk, and a few people, including some of our group, were scattered around the lobby. I remembered Felicia's story about Steve Bloomberg—how he'd written her about the Lenin books she'd left in her car. I wanted to talk to Bloomberg, who supposedly had been with Christina the night she'd drowned.

Monica was talking to BJ about art.

"In our country," she said, "artists either sell out or resign themselves to poverty. Or they commit suicide."

A man I'd never seen before sat next to me and offered me a cigarette. I shook my head.

"Do you find all these militia a bit disconcerting?" the man said in Spanish.

I shrugged. Armed men and women guarded almost every building here against sabotage, and I no longer paid much attention. From my balcony I'd seen the USS *Oxford* patrolling the Florida Straits, so I supposed the Cubans were justified.

"My name is Adolfo," the man now said in English.

I looked at him. He was in his late twenties or early thirties, had dark hair and a thin mustache, and wore the white shirt-jacket that was common in Cuba and which was worn outside the trousers. "And you, Mr. Aucielo, are the journalist from the United States. I am wondering if you would like to see another side of the Cuban Revolution."

Monica was still taking to BJ. "He was an apologist for Stalinism, which is counter-revolutionary." She told BJ a story she'd already told me, a story about the denial of a pair of pants for Osip Mandelstam when the poet was starving and freezing. I remembered that the meanness of this struck Monica as particularly vicious.

"I belong to a group which supports the Revolution," Adolfo told me. "But we have criticisms of certain policies. I wonder if you would you like to meet with us and hear our different point of view regarding the situation in our country."

I shrugged. Everyone else continued with their chattering.

"Maybe the guy was a counter-revolutionary." This was Helen Anderson's voice.

"Stalin had him killed—the greatest Russian poet of the twentieth century!"

"I don't think the Cubans are like that," BJ said.

Adolfo fixed me with a stare. "You are going to meet with Che Guevara tomorrow," he said.

"I don't think so," I replied. "I've already been given the brush-off at the Ministry of Industries."

"One of my friends also has some information about the lady who died in the swimming pool."

"What information?"

Adolfo ignored my question and said, "You and a group of French students are scheduled to meet him at one o'clock. Most of the other offices in the Ministry will be closed for lunch. I think you would find a discussion with me and my friends enlightening and good preparation for this interview. Unfortunately the apartment is small, so only you, please." The Cuban stood up. "Eight o'clock. I'll be at the pool area."

At breakfast a few minutes later, our group was officially informed about the scheduled meeting with Guevara the next day, just as the mysterious Cuban had told me.

There was nothing scheduled for us that afternoon, so Monica and I headed into the city. We took a bus across town, got off at a random stop, and walked together silently. After a while I realized that Monica was guiding me, but I didn't care. Finally, at her suggestion, we stopped at the Bacardi Tasting Room in Old Havana. We'd just gotten inside when the eleven o'clock rain began. It was too early and too warm for me to drink, but Monica didn't hesitate.

"Rum is one of the best things about this country," she said. "By the way, did you notice we're being followed?"

"What?'

"Cubans, CIA, Soviet Intelligence—what's the difference? I'm sure we're probably followed everywhere we go. Let's not talk about that, though. Or about Christina. All right? Let's talk about... I don't know. Are you interested in painting, literature, philosophy? In this heat I get a bit tipsy when I drink."

I said that literature and philosophy were the last things on my mind.

"But have you read Thomas Mann?"

I said I hadn't. I was again surprised by the breadth of Monica's knowledge. She now said that Mann, not Karl Marx, explained what we were seeing in Cuba.

"I mean the mass rallies, Dante, the pressures to conform, belief without questioning, no critical thought."

"These people's lives are changing," I said, automatically taking up the argument. "They're involved in what's happening to them. I thought you were a revolutionary."

"But there's also Freud, who shows us the other side of reason. And the Grand Inquisitor, who tells us that people want bread and security, not freedom."

"If you're trying to get my mind off Christina, it's not working."

The rain stopped. Some old cars and buses passed by, belching smoke.

"You've been contacted by the dissidents," Monica said, suddenly quite sober. "Did they arrange a meeting for you?"

"How—"

"I saw you in the hotel lobby talking to the guy who talked to me. He told me his group is for the Revolution but that they have criticisms. I'd like to hear what they have to say, but to be honest, I don't want to get involved with them. I don't want to drown in some swimming pool. If you meet with them, you'd better be very careful. We're not at home, Dante. Power—now Fidel has it, and he's not going to let it slip out of his hands. So be careful."

"Weren't you telling me on the plane what neat guys Castro and Guevara are?"

"I think Cuba's a mixture of good and some bad. Until there's a revolution led by selfless Buddhists, a lot of this revolutionary talk is just a cover for naked power, whether it's Stalin or Mao or Fidel. And I've been thinking too, and now I don't think Christina's death was an accident."

"Why?"

"You told me before about some Czech she was talking to in Carlsbad, and some guy she was talking to in Paris. I don't think these guys just happened along and said to themselves, 'Why, here's a pretty young American girl—I think I'll tell her my life story. Maybe she'll make it into a movie and take me to Hollywood.'"

"What else?"

"We're followed all the time. Every time I leave the hotel my room gets searched. I think there are more spies than students in our group. But who or what they're spying on, and who they're working for, I don't know."

"What do you know about Campbell and his group?"

"More than I ever wanted to know, and none of it's good. I used to go with a guy named Jeff Green. He'd been a member. He'd also been arrested in Alabama during a voter registration drive and beaten by the local police there. What I'm saying is that Jeff was not the kind of person to tell lies. Anyway, he joined the People's Revolutionary Party because they seemed like the most revolutionary group around. Also they supported the Cuban Revolution. From what Jeff told me, I'd say Jake Campbell is a very shrewd bastard. That printshop you toured in New York? It's not just for printing their own newspaper and pamphlets. They do commercial jobs. Campbell can underbid other companies because his people do all the work, and then they give most of their wages back to the party."

I said I'd already heard this from Art Sparrow.

Monica continued. "They expelled Jeff for raising questions about self-defense in the civil rights movement. He thought that non-violence, as a tactic, would get more support than armed self-defense, which is what Campbell advocates." Monica wasn't drinking any of her rum. "Of course Jake reorganized the leadership with his own people, like Lou Corbett—did you meet him?—and Bloomberg and Helen, who are totally beholden to him. He wouldn't work with Fair Play because we included anybody who supported Cuba. He won't work with anybody who challenges his authority."

"Are you trying to say Campbell might be a killer?"

"He put my friend Jeff on trial for violating party discipline. Campbell said Jeff talked to an outsider about internal party matters. Actually he'd only had a very general discussion with a friend's son about non-violence. Jeff's trial was in some backroom at night. The "comrades" all testified against him. If they'd had the power, Jeff honestly believes they would've shot him. After his expulsion he tried to go into their bookstore one day. They beat him up, broke his arm, and threw him out on the street. They told him next time it would be a knee cap."

I said this was the first I'd heard of Campbell's people using physical violence.

"This woman, Debra Shelton," Monica said. "She was told that if she really believed in the Revolution, she should turn over her trust fund to the party. That's how Campbell gets a lot of money, by the way—trust funds. They took her to meet the grand old man of the party, Tom Kinkaid, and finally got her to give them her money. Later, when she questioned some of Campbell's policies, they said she was a lesbian who had only joined to seduce party women."

These stories sounded to me like miniature versions of the infamous Moscow Trials I'd read about.

"Campbell came into the party with two other guys, Bernie Sobel and Bob Peterson. The three of them went to college together and were called 'the three mouseketeers.' They became the nucleus of the youth group. When Campbell started taking over, the first thing he did was get rid of his old buddies." Monica pushed her drink away. "One of his favorite sayings is that you can't make an omelette without breaking a few eggs."

"Why didn't you tell me any of this earlier, like on our trip across the country?"

"With Anne Montrose listening to everything we said?"

"If you think Campbell and his group are so nasty, why'd you come on this trip?"

"To see Cuba. Che Guevara talks about the possibility of creating a new kind of person—socialist man, if you will, decent human beings. That's what I came to see. But I keep my distance from Campbell and his comrades." She looked at me. "I'm just trying to tell you to be careful."

"You think I should skip this meeting with Adolfo and his friends?"

"They approached me, and I said I'd think about it. I thought you might be interested, so I pointed you out. I'm sorry. This was before Christina's so-called accident. Now I'm scared."

As we stepped out of the air-conditioned tasting room onto the street, we were enveloped in smothering heat.

18

At quarter to eight that night I waited in the lobby of the Havana Riviera for the man who called himself 'Adolfo.' Some of the students were still at dinner and were talking so loudly that I could hear them. Helen walked by, then took the elevator up to the eighteenth floor. I wondered if she was going to search somebody's room. Thornton was playing chess with a woman in militia uniform. Arlene came over to me to say she'd heard that Father Martin had returned from bringing Christina's body to the United States. Sharon and Bloomberg walked quickly through the lobby. I wanted to talk to Sharon, alone, but hadn't yet found an opportunity. Arlene went over to where Thornton was playing chess and sat near him. I guess they'd made up. Monica, BJ, and Art came out of the dining room and headed for the main door. Monica gave me a cautious look.

At eight o'clock, I went out to the swimming pool. The Cuban who called himself 'Adolfo' immediately stepped out of the shadows and told me to follow him. We walked a few blocks to an apartment on the Esplanade. I felt as though I were following my own 'white rabbit' down a dark hole. I had no idea what this guy might lead me into. The building we entered was, like many of the buildings in Havana, in rundown condition—this one had probably been built for tourists in pre-revolutionary times. We climbed the stairs, and Adolfo ushered me into a poorly lit room on the third floor. He introduced me to his friends, six men who only nodded to me. I sat down, was given a cup of coffee, and then, in the dim light, Adolfo began.

"Within the Revolution there are many differences of opinion," he said, speaking in English. "But true democracy is suppressed here. That's the first thing you should ask when you meet with Major Guevara. Ask him why."

Adolfo explained that by 'true democracy,' he meant workers' councils and peasants councils, like in the early Soviet Union. As he talked, I tried to study the faces of the other men. I thought I'd seen one of them at the Union of Artists and Writers. Two of the others had beards. No one was in uniform. But the light was so dim I couldn't see anyone clearly.

The meeting lasted an hour. Adolfo, the only one who spoke, insisted that he and his friends supported the Revolution one hundred percent, but were critical of the authoritarian policies of the Castro brothers and Guevara. This was his main point. He also spoke of differences concerning industrialization, centralized planning, and Russian influence.

"They confiscate our leaflets," he said. "They close down our newspaper. They throw us in jail, then they let us out, then they jail us again. This is all very arbitrary. We also fought in the mountains. We also shed blood. When you meet with Commandante Guevara, ask him about this."

"At the hotel you told me you had information about the American woman who drowned," I said.

"According to the medical report, it was not an accident. She suffered a broken neck before she drowned."

Shocked, trying to understand the import of what this man had just told me, I finally asked Adolfo how he knew this.

"The medical report," he said, and handed it to me. I read through it and then asked if I could take it with me. But Adolfo said that would be too dangerous for him and his group.

I found my own way back to the Havana Riviera. I'd just gotten into my room when there was a knock. It was BJ.

"Got anything to eat?" he said, smiling.

I reached for a bag of cookies I'd bought on the street, and poured us each a rum and Coke.

Standing by the balcony and looking out, BJ said, "Were you in love with Christina?"

"We were friends."

"But you were in love with Felicia."

"Yes."

"I just came by because I thought you might want company."

"I'm okay."

"You're sure? If I can help… if you need anything…"

"Not unless you know something about Christina's accident."

"Just what Sharon said."

I didn't mention to BJ what Adolfo had just told me.

The next morning, I set out to talk to Father Martin, who had accompanied Christina's body back to the States. I found him at the school where he taught. It was in a housing project not far from the hotel. The priest was a tall, soft-spoken man who had reportedly been expelled from Peru for his sympathies with a peasant union. We talked over coffee.

"I wanted to talk to Christina's parents before leaving New York," he said, "but I was told they couldn't be located."

"I think her father might live in Puerto Rico," I said, remembering what Christina had told me. "He's a university teacher."

"No." The priest shook his head. "I got some help from my order. There's nobody teaching there named Ward."

"She was married. Her name was Sanchez, I believe."

"Her passport states her maiden name as Diaz. Apparently she also used the name Sanchez, which might be her mother's name. But, as I say, no relatives could be located."

"Then what happens to her body?"

"I don't know," Father Martin shook his head. "The State Department said they'd handle it."

19

Eleven Americans, two dozen French university students, and two Cubans in military uniforms waited for the Minister of Industries, Ernesto 'Che' Guevara, in his outer office. It was early afternoon and, as usual, very warm. If there was air conditioning, it wasn't working. After several minutes the Commandante arrived, wearing army fatigues. His shirt was unbuttoned at the top. He and two translators sat at the head of a long table. The members of our group and the French students took seats around the table. Behind Guevara, the two men in uniform sat in folding chairs on either side. Guevara leaned forward, propped his elbows on the table, and welcomed us with a smile and a short speech in which he expressed his and his government's condolences for the young North American woman who had sufffered the unfortunate accident. His remarks were translated first into English and then into French. After the translations, he spoke about his concern that the truth of the Cuban Revolution be conveyed to the people of the United States and France.

My first impression was that this man, only a few years older than us, was even more charismatic and handsome than his pictures indicated. During his brief introduction, he even flirted with Monica, Sharon, and the two French girls who were sitting closest to him. As he spoke, I got up and moved around the room, taking pictures. I wanted to ask some of the questions Adolfo had raised, but I was also determined not to let Christina Ward's death be passed over. I was waiting for the right time to confront Guevara, just as I'd confronted Fidel. One of Guevara's assistants, Captain Fuentes, a tall man with a thin mustache, kept a close eye on me, as if he knew what I had in mind.

Jake Campbell asked the first question, which was about Cuba's plans for industrialization.

The minister explained that the industrialization of former colonial countries like Cuba was more complex than he himself had at first realized. Smiling again at the women closest to him, he said that he had personally made many mistakes.

"For example, the manufacture of certain products in Cuba, given the cost of importing raw materials, costs more than the cost of these same products on the world market. The capitalist world division of labor has relegated the countries of Latin America to the role of producing raw materials—in the case of Cuba, sugar and coffee and certain metals. This has to be changed, but, unfortunately, the process of development is difficult."

Taking pictures and taking notes and waiting for an opening to confront Guevara about Christina's death, I wished that I'd at least brought a tape recorder.

Thornton started to ask a question from the other end of the table, but Monica got hers in first. She asked about moral versus material incentives. Guevara said that this issue also was complex. The voluntary work program was not always effective economically. A skilled urban worker might be more valuable working at his trade than, say, cutting sugar cane. But the ideal was valid. A new type of human being was in the process of coming into existence in Cuba. I could see Monica's face light up. This was what she wanted to hear about.

"But we must distinguish between moral incentives and moral pressure," Guevara said. "Moral pressure on the individual, like economic pressure, also creates alienation. We must replace the alienated individual, who in capitalist society produces commodities, by men and women who work for the good of the whole community. Of course, at this stage of history the Revolution demands extraordinary sacrifices." The minister looked at me as I snapped another picture. "But the true revolutionary," he continued, "the vanguard, which is led by Fidel, sets an example for the people as a whole. This is a long process, and we are still in the earliest stages."

Was it socialist man, I wondered, or capitalist man who broke women's necks and drowned them?

"What exactly do you mean, 'replacing' one kind of human being with another?" one of the French students called out in Spanish. "That sounds like a scary proposition."

"People will change through their own actions, as they work to build a truly humane society."

Captain Fuentes was still watching me closely. Otherwise I probably wouldn't have taken notice of him—just another Cuban soldier in uniform and wearing a mustache. I'd seen scores like him. But there was something else, something I couldn't quite place. Had I seen him at Adolfo's secret meeting the other night? I didn't think so. Bloomberg asked something about the subjective factor in history, and Arlene bumped into me in her effort to get closer to the head of the table. Guevara was talking about moving from the "domain of necessity to the realm of freedom." So far none of this stuff would make good newspaper copy.

But the minister now took a range of questions—from guerrilla warfare to the civil rights demonstrations, from the U.S. embargo to the three civil rights workers who'd disappeared in Mississippi and the hypocrisy of the Civil Rights Act signed by President Johnson, from the Baker scandal in the U.S. Senate to the Vietnamese struggle for national liberation, from South African apartheid to the conflict in the Congo. This stuff would make for excellent copy, and I put down my camera to take better notes. Making a point of rejecting "dogmatism and mechanistic thinking" in relation to a question by one of the French students, Guevara was suddenly talking about literature, referring to writers like Cervantes, Goethe, and Neruda.

The guy was well read. I wondered if he'd read that poet Monica was talking about the other day, the one Stalin had sent to Siberia for the crime of writing a satirical poem.

During our other interviews with government officials—who had all spoken in clichés and platitudes—our group had often showed signs of boredom after just a few minutes. Now even Sharon Albright, who would usually be squirming in her chair, seemed alert and anxious to participate in the discussion.

Guevara obviously liked his audience. The half hour we'd been allotted had long since passed. As I looked around the room, I wondered what Che saw. Did he see Campbell as I saw him, as a self-important leader of a tiny radical party with its dogmatic followers and a few other privileged young Americans? But due to the seriousness with which Che responded to each question, and because he was never patronizing, I wondered if he saw the potential, even here, of the new, better human being he'd referred to earlier. At one point, during a discussion about stages of development and whether a democratic or Socialist revolution was on the agenda for Latin America, Campbell asked if Guevara's statements weren't somewhat "Trotskyite."

Guevara said that one needed to answer arguments with other arguments and with reasons, not just with labels. Campbell seemed taken aback, as if Guevara had just uttered a great blasphemy.

As the only journalist present—as the reporter whose stories and photos were being picked-up by newspapers in North America—I thought the minister was paying special attention to me. He would look at me as if he wanted to make sure that I wrote down exactly what was being said. But perhaps each of us was feeling this way. A tall Frenchman, who had gotten up and was now standing closer to Guevara, asked in French about artistic freedom.

"For the individual in capitalist society," the minister said, leaning back in his chair and puffing on his cigar, "art represents an escape. Artistic freedom is often a disguise for escapism. Unfortunately, socialist countries have often opposed this escapism with dogmatism—and with a kind of scholasticism. This has resulted in a mechanical realism, called 'socialist realism.' The aim of the party in Cuba is to educate the people. To do this, free artistic inquiry is needed, but also socialist consciousness." He looked at the people around the table. "I think great artists will appear to the degree that the field of culture, and the possibilities for expression, are broadened."

The Frenchman who had asked about artistic freedom immediately asked who would determinine if an artist had the "proper socialist consciousness." Che's answer, "the people," didn't satisfy seem to satisfy this man, who wanted to continue the discussion. He tried to ask about freedom of the press, but one of our group, Steve Bloomberg, interrupted.

"Would Cuba," Bloomberg said, "help other countries fight against imperialism?"

"Revolution," Guevara said, "is the duty of all who claim to be revolutionaries."

Was this an answer or just another slogan? I wondered.

I was getting anxious about asking my questions before the session ended. Somebody asked in French about the relationship between central planning and self-management of individual enterprises, and a complicated discussion ensued. Che was now talking about the need for social good to take precedence over the law of value, or over profit—an issue of interest to economists, I supposed. But I wanted to know about a murder. I decided this was the time to ask my own questions, but before I could, another French student asked, "Why are you suppressing other Cuban revolutionaries?"

The room fell silent. Except for Thornton's outburst earlier, this was the first real confrontation.

The French student continued in Spanish. "I'm specifically referring to revolutionaries who also fought to overthrow Batista but who have differences of opinion with the leaders of your government."

I realized that this person must also have talked to Adolfo and his friends, for it was one of the questions they had wanted me to ask.

"As our revolution moved into its socialist phase," Guevara said, "we left behind many, who then became counter-revolutionaries and began to attack us and tried to sabotage—"

"I'm talking about revolutionary socialists," the student said. I was only a few feet from the minister and was still holding my camera. "You confiscate their newspapers and leaflets and throw them in jail. But these are Cubans who support the Revolution, people who have shed their blood for the Revolution."

The soldier on Guevara's left, Captain Lima, a man with graying hair whose eyes had almost been closed, sat up in his chair. On the other side, a few feet behind the minister, Captain Fuentes, lean and dark, put his cigarette out, stood up, and moved to the side of the room. I still couldn't remember where I'd seen him before.

Nobody interrupted the French student. He continued, "They have criticisms of the leadership and want to express their views. Didn't Marx write that socialism, based on a just distribution of goods, would be an extension of democracy?"

"Within the limits of support for the Revolution, everything is open for debate and discussion," Guevara said. "But we have not yet perfected forms of socialist democracy. There have been bureaucratic abuses. And of course we are still being attacked almost daily by our imperialist enemies."

Monica now joined the debate. "That's how the Soviet Union has justified its ban on factions and its totalitarian rule for almost half a century," she said.

"Some of these so-called revolutionaries," Che replied, "believe that socialism will be constructed on the ashes of nuclear war. Of course, they are entitled to their views." I saw the minister gesture to his assistants, Captains Fuentes and Lima, to let the discussion continue.

"Does that mean anyone who disagrees with the leadership is a counter-revolutionary?" another French student asked.

Thornton spoke up now. "What good is it if a man gain the world and lose his soul? What good are these housing projects and factories if you don't allow democracy?"

Guevara was calm. "The United States, for example, claims to be democratic. But the U.S. government denies the most basic rights to its black citizens, and would deny Cuba and Vietnam and other underdeveloped countries the right to determine their own destinies."

"When will Cuba institute democratic forms?" Monica asked.

"When will Cubans get to vote and organize political parties?" the French student asked.

"We do not accept the empty forms of bourgeois democracy. You must see for yourself the dialectic between Fidel and the masses before you judge us. On 26 July, over a million Cubans, armed Cubans, will fill the Plaza of the Revolution. They will have rifles, loaded rifles. Any one of them could shoot Fidel, or me, or any or all of our leaders. That is democracy in action."

Somebody said in English that she didn't think that a mass rally, even of armed people, was much of a substitute for elections. Then Monica said that Che hadn't really answered her question. I thought she was right, and wondered how aware Guevara was of his own contradictions. I saw that several of the French students, and at least four of our group—

Monica, Art, Thornton, and I—weren't satisfied with Guevara's concept of democracy. I wondered if he was expressing the same elitism that was typical of organizations like the People's Revolutionary Party. What would Che himself do, I wanted to ask, if he found himself on the losing side of the debates now going on in Cuba? But before I could ask this, a French woman shouted out, "Do you believe in terrorism? How many hundreds of people has your government executed?"

"After the Revolution, many of Batista's murderers and torturers were put on trial," Che Guevara, who had conducted those trials, said. "Those who were found guilty of terrible crimes against the Cuban people were executed. They also have capital punishment in the United States, but it is directed against the poor, especially the Negro. In Cuba it is used against those who attack our citizens."

The French girl was ready to continue her attack, but Sharon Albright brought unexpected levity to the interview by now asking how Che had gotten the name of "Che." There was laughter. Again flirting, Che explained that this was a nickname.

With Sharon's question and the laughter, the room settled down. There were a few more questions, nothing controversial. But instead of half an hour, the interview had gone on for well over two hours. The minister now went around the room and took final questions. He didn't respond to any of the thirty or so questions until all of them had been asked. Then he went around the room again, and, directing himself to the person who had asked the question, gave his answer. After his last question, he stood up and thanked us for coming to Cuba. He was about to leave when I finally asked my question.

"Mr. Minister," I said. "One last question, please. One of our group, Christina Ward, died a few nights ago." Guevara nodded slightly, as if to say he'd already expressed his regrets. "This death is being called an accident," I continued. "But it was not an accident. I would like to know why the Cuban government is calling Christina Ward's death an accident when your own medical examiners have stated that it was not."

Now chaos broke out. Everybody spoke at once—in English, Spanish, and French—shouting at each other and at me and at God knows what else.

Guevara held up his hand, and the room fell silent.

"I'm sorry. I don't know the circumstances or any details," he said in Spanish, looking at me. "But I promise that we will look into this." Then, thanking us again for coming to Cuba, and flanked by his two assistants, he left the room.

20

It took me a few moments to gather my cameras and notebook, and so I was one of the last to leave the conference room. Before I reached the door, I felt a hand on my arm. It was one of Guevara's assistants, Captain Lima, who had been sitting behind Che Guevara during the interview. Older than the typical Cuban soldier, he was a short, thin man with gray in his hair and a Castillian accent. If I would remain for a few minutes, he whispered, the Commandante wished to speak to me privately. Captain Lima closed the door, and I went back to the table and sat down. A few minutes later Guevara returned. After a polite inquiry about my reactions to the Cuban Revolution, he asked, in English, the reasons for my suspicions about Christina Ward's death.

Although I didn't say where I'd gotten this information, I said I'd learned about the conclusions of the medical examination which had been performed in Cuba. Guevara looked over at his assistant.

Guevara looked at me steadily and spoke almost in a whisper. "I met Miss Ward earlier this year, when she came to arrange for your tour. You understand that almost daily we are being attacked and must therefore be very vigilant. For example, there have already been several attempts on Fidel's life." He looked very tired. "During the course of your group's visit, Miss Ward was observed meeting with people who have been under suspicion but who so far have been allowed to continue their activities."

I'd already heard—from Christina herself and then from Jake Campbell—so many stories about her that I didn't know what to believe. Now Che Guevara was implying that she was involved in "suspicious" activities. Was this the reason for the suppression of the medical examiner's report? The minister asked if there was anything I could tell the Cuban authorities that might help them. I realized they must know about my meeting with Adolfo and his friends. Did this mean I was under suspicion too? I said I couldn't think of anything. Guevara then asked me to be patient and allow the Cuban government to continue its investigation.

"And you want me to hold off writing a newspaper story," I said.

Guevara smiled. "Not at all." He stood. "Captain Lima will keep you informed."

21

Back in my hotel room, I poured myself a rum and Coke. Then I decided I'd better not drink it, because I needed to think. First, what did this mean about Christina? There had been her meeting with Bertrand in Paris and with Hutoc in Czechoslovakia, but whom had she been meeting with in Cuba? It was then that I remembered where I'd seen Che Guevara's other assistant, the one with the mustache, Captain Fuentes. I wasn't really sure, but I thought I might have taken his picture. I got out my stacks of contact prints and began digging through them. I didn't see Fuentes the first time through. There were some photos that I must have picked up by mistake at the Prensa office, and these had gotten mixed up with my own. They looked like police photos, pictures of an old man being booked. I pulled them out and put them in my camera bag to give to Jose Zambala at the Prensa office. But on my second pass through the contact sheets, I held a magnifying glass over some of the group shots and looked at them more closely, especially shots of our group's arrival at the Jose Marti Airport, at a group shot with President Dorticos, and at some photos I'd taken of the group on the steps of Havana University. From this last set of photos, I honed in on one particular shot. Then I found the roll of film it had come from and developed the picture I wanted.

And there he was, Captain Fuentes. It was a picture I'd taken at the University of Havana. He was on the group's right, in back. The reason I'd noticed him was probably because he was standing next to Christina Ward. This was interesting but not unusual or suspicious. Christina was pretty. It was natural for her to attract men. What was disturbing was that Fuentes turned up in another photo, one I'd taken during our visit to the new art school. And, again, he was next to Christina. In this photo they seemed to be talking. But did this mean they were conspiring? More likely it meant that Fuentes had been trying to date Christina.

I picked up the rum and Coke I'd poured and took a sip. Then I set the glass on the coffee table and walked out on the balcony to look out at the Malecon and the sea, and to think. Perhaps if I hadn't been so preoccupied I might have noticed that the balcony railing had come loose from the building. As I leaned against it, it gave way.

I went over the side. I grabbed onto a piece of iron and swung away from the building. I was eighteen floors above the ground. I shouted for help. The balconies to the left and right of my mine were empty. I shouted again. Somebody came onto a balcony. It was Frank Vara, who leaped over to my balcony, reached down, and hauled me to safety. Out of breath, and suddenly exhausted and trembling, I sort of rolled back into the hotel room.

"What happened?" Vara said.

I told him. He went out on the balcony. Then he came back inside and said, "I think the bolts which hold the railing to the building came out."

"You saved my life."

"May I?" He pointed to the bottle of rum, and poured us both drinks. I had barely touched the drink I'd poured before going out on the balcony. Now I drank both of them.

There was a knock on the door. It was Monica. Vara told her what had happened. Then BJ knocked and came in.

"These buildings haven't had much upkeep in the past few years," Vara said.

Monica said, "You could've been killed!"

BJ went out to look at the broken railing. "Jesus," he said when he came back inside.

I thanked everybody for their concern. Monica poured us all another drink. When she and BJ left, Vara stayed behind.

"Thanks again," I said.

"I'll tell maintenance about the railing," Vara said, and left.

Cautiously I went out on the balcony and looked at the bolts which had come loose, and the hole they'd left in the wall of the building. I didn't believe this was an accident. I'd already caught Helen Anderson in my room. Then somebody, maybe Helen but maybe someone else, had set the timer on my camera to take pictures of me. How many people were sneaking in and out this room? But why would somebody want to kill me? I went back inside, loaded the timer camera with film, set the timer, and put the camera on the mantle.

22

In the morning, after delivering my story and pictures of the interview with Che Guevara to the Prensa office, I headed for the apartment where I'd met with Adolfo and the other dissidents. It was only after I was several blocks away from the office that I remembered the photos I'd put in my camera bag and meant to return to Jose Zambala. At the apartment building, unsure of quite what to do, I waited across the street and watched for anyone who might be following me. I didn't see anyone. Finally I crossed the street, climbed the staircase, and knocked. A woman in an army uniform answered. I asked for Adolfo. The woman said I had the wrong apartment. All I could think to do was identify myself and say that if she saw Adolfo, to have him contact the North American reporter. The woman stared at me without speaking, and I left.

At the hotel I was told our group would be leaving Havana in two days for our tour of the island. Since we'd be coming back to Havana for the July 26th celebration and would have the same rooms at the hotel, we didn't need to pack all our things. This would be especially convenient for me because of the dark room I'd set up. I wanted to pack up my contact sheets and negatives, and store them at the Prensa office, but Campbell stopped me. He was anxious to talk, and we went to my room.

"I think you're letting that unfortunate accident cloud your reason," he said, sitting down and offering me a Cuban cigar. "First you attack Fidel Castro. Then you attack Che Guevara."

I refused the cigar and sat across from him.

"Let me tell you a few things you might not be aware of, Aucielo. To begin with, Christina liked to glamorize herself. But the reality of her life wasn't very glamorous." Campbell now told me that Christina Ward's mother had been an alcoholic, and that Christina had been an alcoholic when she was a teenager, and that when someone who has not been drinking for years suddenly falls off the wagon, especially in extreme summer heat, they can get fatally intoxicated.

"Her mother's still an alcoholic. Chrissy had once been an alcoholic. You don't get over that. It was the party that changed her life. As I told you before, I met her at City College, where I was speaking. She came to some meetings and eventually joined us. I think she was ashamed of her background, because she created another life for herself—this glamorous personal history she made up. And earlier this year she came with me to Cuba to set up this trip, because she was very good at languages. I don't know who else she might have gotten involved with. What I'm trying to say is that Christina Ward wasn't all that she said she was. She was capable of doing some outrageous things, like getting drunk and then going for a swim."

"Or getting involved with strange people?"

"I just wanted you to consider these things when you write about her death. Because as soon as you imply foul play, the Cubans, and us, the People's Revolutionary Party, are going to be blamed."

"Did you know her neck was broken?"

Campbell took the cigar out of his mouth and stared at me. "How do you know that?"

"Just take my word for it."

"I guess she fell."

"And broke her neck? Where did she fall from, the roof of the hotel?"

Campbell was silent for a minute.

"And Sharon Albright's story?" I said. "Is that true?"

"Sharon was also drunk that night. She told us what happened as she remembers it."

I said, "Did you know Father Martin couldn't locate Christina's parents in New York?"

Campbell shrugged.

"Did you ever meet her husband?"

"I think he lives in Brooklyn. No, I've never met him. They were already separated when she came around the party."

"Is this all you wanted to tell me?" I said. "That Christina's background wasn't exactly what she said it was?"

"Listen, I'm as sorry about what happened as anybody. She was more than a friend and comrade. But, you know, the Kennedy assassination has spawned millions of conspiracy nuts. I didn't think you were one of them." Campbell got up. At the door, he turned and started to speak, but apparently changed his mind and left.

It was probably for the best that he left, because I knew he was lying, again, and I didn't know if I could control my anger. The notion that Christina Ward—or Sanchez or Diaz or whatever—could be an alcoholic was just too preposterous.

Ten minutes later I had another visitor, Dick Thornton.

"You think any more about China?" he said.

"No."

"I got another proposition for you. But it ain't free. It's a trade. My information in exchange for that interview I asked about before."

"What've you got?"

"I want that interview—Black Nationalist views on the Cuban Revolution."

"I can write it up and send it in, but I can't promise it'll be published."

"That's good enough." Thornton sat down, crossed his legs, leaned back, and smiled. "It's about Christina Ward. I don't know exactly what happened to her. But I do know what didn't happen. That story Sharon told about her and Christina in the swimming pool? I do know that ain't true."

"How do you know that?"

"That night I saw Sharon going into Steve Bloomberg's room. I was watching because I thought Arlene was in there with him. I'm in the room next door, and I hear Bloomberg and Sharon. The glass doors to the balcony were open in his room and in mine."

"I heard you accused Arlene of being with Bloomberg that night."

"I was just trying to get her to confess. I don't know where she was. But don't tell me Sharon Albright was with Christina Ward in the swimming pool because I heard her with Arthur Sparrow."

"I thought you said Bloomberg."

"That's what I meant. Steve Bloomberg." Thornton laughed. "She used to be a nun. Did you know that? Sharon a nun—what a laugh!"

Like Thornton being a preacher, I thought. But if he was right, then

Campbell had gotten Sharon Albright to lie, maybe to cover his own involvement. What had Felicia and Christina done that had put their lives in danger? Both the Cubans and the People's Revolutionary Party were embarrassed by Christina's death. Jake Campbell had been angry about Felicia's Cuba trip. If he'd been involved in Felicia's death, and if Christina had learned about it... And Campbell had denied knowing either Bertrand or Hutoc. But if he was telling the truth about Bertrand and Hutoc, then who exactly was Christina Ward? I needed to talk to the mysterious Cuban, Adolfo, about Christina.

A message was waiting at the desk when I came down to the lobby. Mrs. Wilson wanted more information on the drowning accident and more particulars about Christina Ward. Since we would soon be leaving Havana for our tour of the island, and we'd all be riding on one bus, I thought I'd try to talk to Sharon Albright—by herself, without Campbell or anyone else coaching her—as soon as possible.

23

Sharon Albright was pretty but a bit on the dull side. Thornton was right—it was difficult to believe she'd ever been a nun. I found her in the hotel lobby, waiting for Helen Anderson. When I approached, she told me they were going to see a movie at the Cinemateca, which was not far from the hotel.

"I love old movies," she said, as if there wasn't enough to see in Cuba. This was a double-bill, *The Beast with Five Fingers* and *King Soloman's Mines*. I told Sharon I was on my way to see the same show and would like to go with her and Helen. I said I'd call Helen's room and tell her to hurry so we wouldn't miss the beginning of the movie. As Sharon watched, I picked up the desk phone and pretended to talk into it. Then I told Sharon that Helen said for us to go ahead and she'd meet us at the theater.

The Cinemateca, a small, new building, was empty except for us. The first thing that came on was a Cuban newsreel featuring... ourselves, playing ping-pong with Fidel. Seeing myself on the screen, I had a feeling of unreality. Then came the main feature, an old horror movie which involved a severed hand with a life of its own. It was seeking revenge against somebody. I closed my eyes and remembered how as a kid I'd gone to the movies every Saturday. The price then was twenty cents—until I discovered the fire escape hatch on the roof of the movie theater. Then I'd climb up the fire escape, lift the fire hatch on the roof, and climb down a long metal ladder into the dark theater which ended on the stage behind the screen. From there I'd sneak into the auditorium. I remembered how, as I climbed down that ladder, my own shadow would be thrown onto the image the movie made on a concrete wall behind the screen. I remembered my shadow, as I climbed down that ladder. It resembled a fly crawling over the giant faces in the movie. Sitting next to Sharon Albright as the beast with five fingers wreaked its vengeance, I wondered if that was what I was now, the shadow of an insect amongst larger-than-life giants. When Sharon put her hand on my arm, I opened my eyes and watched the movie for awhile. Then I remembered another scene from my movie-going childhood. The balcony of the neighborhood theater had been where my first teen-age sexual encounters had taken place. I would ask a girl if she had a match, and if she responded favorably, I'd sit next to her and put my arm around her.

I didn't need to ask Sharon for a match. She was already leaning against me. I decided one movie was enough, and we walked back to the hotel, her hand on my arm—the way Christina had held onto me on this same street. Sharon wondered what had happened to Helen. Not wanting to rush things by asking questions too soon, I let her talk. In fact, she couldn't stop talking. She was going on and on about the *Beast with Five Fingers*. Then she told me about *The Creature from the Black Lagoon*, and a movie about giant ants, and other horror movies. When we got up to my room, she casually took off her blouse and skirt and began talking about her days in the convent. She'd been very unhappy there. It had been like a horror movie. I poured drinks. Sharon had left the convent in search of love. What did I think about that, about her being in a convent? Did I remember Lucille Ball's Latin Lover, Desi Arnez? He was the most famous Cuban in the world. Carmen Miranda—did I remember her? She was the one with fruit piled on her head. Sharon thought that Desi Arnez was a cross between The Cisco Kid and Pancho. She loved Rita Moreno and Fernando Lamas and Ricardo something-or-other. She picked up our drinks and took them into the bedroom. I watched as she got into my bed. She had a terrific body. Anthony Quinn was Mexican. Did I know that? As I sipped my drink, I listened to Sharon Albright's life history.

After the convent she'd lived in Greenwich Village. But the bohemians were phony. Didn't I agree? Had I seen *King Soloman's Mines*? It was a great movie. We should go back and see it sometime.

To make conversation I said, "As long as the Cuban Revolution was another Hollywood adventure movie, it was acceptable. But when the Cubans turned out to be real human beings, and their revolution was the real thing, I guess they were no longer acceptable."

"What?"

"I said—"

"Can I have another drink?"

As I went for the bottle of rum, I asked what her life had been like before the convent.

"My parents were separated," Sharon said. She was lying on the bed. I sat on the edge, still dressed. "I lived with my mother in Brooklyn and New Jersey until I was fifteen. I was already pretty developed. I started going out with men in their twenties and thirties. At fifteen, with make-up and all dressed up, I could pass for twenty-five. One day my mother found the clothes I used for dates. She accused me of being a whore and started beating me. Later, when I was sleeping, she started talking very quietly and asked where I'd gotten the clothes. I told her a boy I was dating gave them to me. Then she pushed my face into the pillow and punched me. She pulled all my clothes out of the closet and tried to tear them up."

Sharon stopped. I asked her to continue.

"The next day we drove to school to talk to my teachers. But my mother started screaming before we got to the building. I was never so humiliated in my life. Kids were laughing, others were swearing at my mother, the rest just watched. I could never accept that those kids, who I thought were my friends, could watch me getting hit and screamed at and not do anything."

Sharon was drunk now. She held tightly onto my arm.

"My mother drove me out of Newark. I asked where we were going. She said it was a surprise. We parked by a lake or reservoir, and she told me she was going to kill me. She yanked off the scarf I was wearing and tightened it until I couldn't breathe. Then she stopped and asked if I'd had enough. But when I got my breath, I kicked, and somehow I got the car door open, and I ran. The police took me to a home where I stayed until my father came."

Sharon was crying. I held her. It was after this experience that she'd gone into the convent. I felt for her, but I had to ask her about Christina and the swimming pool.

I said, "Sharon, why did you lie about Christina being drunk at the pool? Were you even there?"

"Jake said we have to protect the party and support the Revolution."

"Were you and she even at the pool together?"

"Earlier, but she wasn't swimming." Sharon's eyes were closing. Softly she said, "Steve and I left. She got drunk and went swimming after we left. So it wasn't much of a lie."

Sharon's eyes closed. I let her sleep and went down to the lobby. When I came back, she was gone.

24

Everybody was lying—Campbell, Sharon Albright, the Cubans—I didn't know if I'd ever find out the truth about Christina's death. Since we were scheduled to leave on our tour of the island the next day, we were given time to relax. Monica invited me to go with her to visit Ernest Hemingway's famous house, the Finca, outside Havana.

We took a bus to the ferry, crossed the harbor, and then boarded a bus. On the bus I told Monica about Sharon Albright's confession—although I didn't say how I'd gotten it.

At the Finca, a middle-aged guide who had once been Hemingway's houseboy showed us around the grounds and the house. Almost every wall was adorned with the heads of horned animals. The guide pointed out the writing desk where "Papa" had stood every morning to work. In the courtyard was a tower which had been built for the writers's privacy but which he'd seldom used. I liked Hemingway's stories, but I wondered if the writer had been just another rich American taking advantage of a poor country. He apparently lived in an exclusive world of private beaches, yacht clubs, casinos, and bars. But maybe *The Old Man and the Sea* redeemed his life in Cuba.

While Monica went on with the tour, I went out to the garden which surrounded the compound. I was alone, far away from the house, when suddenly a man stepped out from a tree in front of me. It was Adolfo, the dissident who had taken me to meet his friends and who had given me questions to ask Che Guevara. Seeing my reaction, he apologized for scaring me.

The Cuban said, "Guevara is taking your accusations very seriously. People high up in the government are trying to find out what's going on, but other people are trying to keep this thing quiet because they don't want bad publicity."

"What can you tell me about Captain Fuentes?" I said.

"Fuentes? Why do you ask about Fuentes?"

I told him about the photos I had of Fuentes and Christina Ward.

Looking around the garden to make sure we were alone, Adolfo said, "Che trusts him, but Che trusts many people he perhaps shouldn't trust."

"I need to know something, Adolfo—or whatever your name is. What was your relationship with Christina Ward?"

"I did not know the lady. The one you are with today—I've talked to her. Listen. Do not go to my apartment again. It's too dangerous, for me and for you. The government believes Christina Ward was trying to smuggle something out of the country."

I stared at the Cuban.

"I don't know what it was. Believe me. I and my friends are loyal. I don't know who she was working with, but not any of us." The Cuban reached out to shake my hand. "We must be careful," he said, and disappeared.

25

Our bus tour of the island took us east, towards Santiago at the other end of Cuba. Each day we visited state or cooperative farms, fishing cooperatives, schools, or factories. There were inspirational meetings at every stop, vanguard workers who praised us as revolutionary comrades, and provincial officials who declared us heroes. And at each of these meeting I dutifully took pictures—of the Cubans and of my fellow travelers, one or more of whom, I believed, was a murderer.

As we jouneyed across the long, narrow island, I found myself comparing this trip to my recent trip across the United States. In Cuba we talked to everyone we could, asking questions and even raising arguments, whereas on the drive from Berkeley to New York we'd kept to ourselves, avoiding arguments or even speaking with people in the restaurants and cafes we'd stopped at. It was bad enough, Anne Montrose had said, that six young people were driving through the country with California license plates. We'd carefully observed all speed limits and suppressed our reactions to the racist comments we heard about civil rights demonstrators. We'd kept our mouths shut as the good Christian people in the heart of America expressed their hatred of blacks, describing them as "ungrateful niggers" who ignorantly followed Communist agitators like Martin Luther King.

Still, I wondered what the Cubans were not telling or showing us. Somewhere they had prisons for counter-revolutionaries, but who exactly was considered counter-revolutionary? According to Che Guevara, people who were "for" the Revolution were okay. But who made this determination? What about people in the provinces who were critical of the Revolution? So far I hadn't met any.

Campbell and his comrades, including Sharon, now avoided me. There was no mention of Christina by any of them. Since there were only eleven of us now, there was plenty of room for the comrades to sit by themselves and have their private meetings, which they often did.

"Conditions are usually worse in the countryside," Art said as we passed fields of sugar cane. "During Mao's 'Great Leap Forward,' the peasants starved by the millions."

"Because a government calls itself 'Communist' or 'Socialist' doesn't mean it is," Monica said.

"But life for the average Chinese has improved under Mao," Bloomberg answered from several seats behind us.

Monica, who never ducked a fight, turned around. "How would you know? Even during Stalin's collectivization and purges there were plenty of intellectuals from the West who visited the Soviet Union and returned singing its praises."

Helen Anderson shouted, "If the Socialist bloc is so bad, and the advanced capitalist countries are bad, then what does Miss Know-It-All propose?"

"Cuba's different," Maria Montalvo, our guide, said softly. Usually Ricardo and Maria acted as if they didn't hear our discussions, and only spoke when asked questions or when translating. They were now sitting with Frank Vara in the middle of the bus, between the four party members and the other six of us.

"Yes," Sharon called out. "Cubans are very open."

BJ Johnson said, "The Soviets and the Chinese may have screwed up. But I think Cuban socialism is different."

"He who pays the piper calls the tune, and the Russians are paying," Monica said. She thought that BJ was secretly a member of the PRP, and had already told him he ought to be sitting with his comrades.

"What about Che?" Steve Bloomberg said. "And Fidel? Don't you think they're different?"

"I'd say Che's the most open-minded government official we've seen so far," Monica answered. "But I wouldn't be surprised to hear that he dies in a plane accident or something like that."

"Didn't you like Fidel?" Sharon asked.

"He didn't say much, did he? He played ping-pong with us. Have you noticed that every time any of us asks about democracy, we're told that Fidel listens to the people? All right, granted that he does. But is that democracy or is it a benevolent dictatorship?"

Monica had told me she thought it was only a matter of time before Adolfo and his friends, as well as any other critics of the regime, were imprisoned.

"Because eventually Castro has to let them organize openly and legally and publish their newspaper," she'd told me. "Or else he'll have to suppress them completely. We're still—every one of us—being followed everywhere, at all times."

Art was even harsher in his estimate of freedom in Cuba. "Castro has everyone spying on everyone else," he maintained.

Our bus broke down three times, and we had to wait on the side of the road while repairs were made. Fortunately the bus driver was a good mechanic and had spare parts and spare tires. As we traveled, I took photographs of barns and sheds, many of which were decorated with slogans like "Venceremos" and "Patria o Muerte." I was especially fascinated by the juxtaposition of the new and the old, and I took photos of newly built bridges next to dirt roads, children in their schools next to fields where peasants cut cane with machetes, concrete buildings next to old shacks, horses and mules alongside Soviet-made tractors. And as we traveled across the island, Monica, Art, Thornton, and I continued to raise the issue of democracy at every stop we made. But all we got from the factory and farm managers were the same stock answers. Whenever any of us brought up anything critical, Campbell and the comrades, including BJ, were sure to answer us with a speech in support of the Revolution.

Because of the narrowness of the island, I could sometimes see the Atlantic on one side and mountains on the other. No wonder Cuba had been a tourist resort. In spite of the heat, it was a beautiful place. I might have enjoyed this trip if I hadn't been haunted by two deaths. I kept going back to the night Christina had come to my room, the night she'd heard the camera with the timer clicking every ten minutes. And I thought about the second time she'd come, when she'd used my bathroom and then, hurriedly, left. I asked Art and Monica what they thought about these visits.

"She was in the bathroom for a really long time," I said. "She said she wasn't feeling well. Then she just left. What I'm wondering is whether she was looking for something in my bathroom. Because that's where my photos are, all my negatives and contact prints." I had in mind the photos showing her and Captain Fuentes, but I didn't mention these. I wondered if she'd thought I'd taken pictures of something secret. When we got back to Havana, I'd look through all my pictures again.

Because the Cubans were letting us keep the same rooms at the Havana Riviera, I hadn't dismantled my bathroom photo lab, but I had stored my developed photos, my contact prints, and my negatives at the Prensa office for safekeeping. I wondered if Cuban agents were there now, looking through them.

26

The bus trip already seemed endless—field after field of sugar cane, the sea coast, bridges, rivers and gorges, the deep browns and greens of the Cuban earth, isolated shacks, peasants carrying loads along the road. We stopped in Camaguey, in Santa Clara. Campbell and his comrades spoke to each other in whispers. Thornton complained about the heat and the food, and Arlene apologized for him. Of course, Thornton was right. The food wasn't always very good, and we were often kept waiting, and the bus was too hot, and our accommodations were sometimes cramped and dirty. But by Cuban standards we were living high on the hog.

Maria and Ricardo did their best to explain the difficulties, but they were clearly frustrated with us. Maria told Monica and me how Yankees had used her country as a playground and had corrupted Cubans with dollars. Now, I thought, after five years of not seeing decadent Americans, we had come, the "heroic" students, as if to remind Cubans of North American values.

Monica thought that the Cubans were probably also offended that their guests were jumping in and out of each other's beds and getting drunk whenever possible. And both Monica and I thought that Maria must be losing patience with Campbell, who was still trying to seduce her.

I wondered what Maria and Ricardo would have thought if I'd told them they were riding a bus and sharing meals with a murderer.

We were taken to the Bay of Pigs, and the 1961 invasion was described in detail. We saw the swamp where Fidel had landed in the Granma. But it was clear to me that the group had had enough sightseeing, and that any of us would have preferred the swimming pool at the Havana Riviera.

The party comrades began shunning Richard Thornton, and Thornton in turn stopped speaking to everyone except Arlene Washington and sometimes me. Sharon and BJ sat and ate together. And Art, Monica, and I mostly talked to each other.

Before reaching Santiago, we spent a full day at a school city in one of the most inaccessible parts of the Sierra Maestra Mountains. This was where Fidel had established his first guerrilla base. I took pictures from the back of the heavy-duty Russian truck which carried us up the mountain.

We had to walk the last few hundred yards to the school city. We'd already seen hundreds of children in uniform, singing and repeating revolutionary songs and phrases. But these kids were different, local kids who a few years earlier would have been condemned to the most abysmal poverty. I took dozens of pictures of them and their young teachers. BJ told me he wanted to stay in Cuba and work in a place like this.

After dinner I skipped the speeches and student performances and went to the room Art and I were sharing. My photos were in Havana, but I did have my notebooks, and I looked up the first interview I'd had with Christina Ward in Berkeley. I had four notebooks written in my own shorthand. They included my interviews and notes on the trip, including what I'd written about the drive across the U.S. and our stays in Paris and Czechoslovakia.

I was now struck by something in my first interview with Christina Ward in Berkeley. My question: What's your relationship to the trip planned by Felicia Vasquez and the Fair Play for Cuba Committee? Christina's answer: That trip was cancelled.

Christina had gone on to say that she'd made arrangements for the People's Revolutionary Party trip in January of this year. But in January Felicia's trip had not been cancelled. It hadn't been "cancelled" until Felicia had been "cancelled" three months later. Had this just been a mistake on Christina's part? Or had Felicia's trip, and Felicia, already been "cancelled" in some way as early as January? I wondered if Ricardo or Maria, our guides, had been part of the January discussions with Campbell and Christina. I found Maria drinking tea with a group of teachers in their barracks. She introduced me to her comrades, who were all dressed in army fatigues, and offered me a cup of tea.

"You missed the wonderful speeches of our honor students," she said.

"Maria, I'm working on an article, and I thought you might be able to help."

We stepped outside the barracks. The mountain air was clear and cold, the night full of stars.

"Do you remember when Christina Ward came to Cuba to make arrangements for this trip?"

"Yes. She and Jacob came early this year. We had a meeting at the University."

"So you were going to have two American groups this summer."

"No, just this one, I believe."

"Wasn't there another trip scheduled by a group called Fair Play for Cuba?"

"You're right. But the other trip was called off."

"Did you meet the lady who was organizing that first trip?" I asked.

"I was introduced to her. A lovely woman."

Like the woman I was now talking to, I thought. But had Felicia's trip been cancelled only after she was killed, or had it already been cancelled, in some way, back in January? I didn't know if this was important, and I didn't know how I could find out.

Art was reading a chess book when I returned to the room. He put down the book. "The kids sang and performed," he said. "It was very nice. How about a game of chess?"

"Art, weren't you supposed to go on the Fair Play trip to Cuba?"

"Yes, but after the Kennedy assassination and allegations that Oswald was involved with Fair Play and that Cuba might be involved, there were problems. Fair Play was thinking about postponing the trip. And then, of course, Felicia died."

"And when she died, you were contacted by Christina Ward and the People's Revolutionary Party."

"Actually the Committee to Uphold the Right to Travel. I think all the people who had signed up with Felicia were contacted."

"Except the Trotskyites."

"Well, one of them seems to have sneaked aboard."

I knew he meant Monica, but he was wrong. She didn't belong to any group. She was just a socialist who hated Stalinism.

The next morning the entire school city, students and teachers, lined up on both sides of the dirt road and waved to us as we went back down the mountain.

We arrived in Santiago that afternoon. After lunch at a fishing cooperative, we were taken to a small hotel outside the city. The place reminded me of the sort of motel I'd seen on the drive across America. It even had a pint-sized swimming pool—hopefully too small for anyone to drown in. As usual, Art and I shared a room. There was a festival going on, and most of our group immediately headed into town. I found a café and was working on an article about the school city when Arlene came in.

"You've got to come back to the hotel," she said, out of breath. "Richard needs you."

Thornton was in his room. Two plainclothes Cubans who identified themselves as policemen were standing outside the motel. Thornton told me they'd been questioning him.

"There's an American woman who came to Cuba with her boyfriend and works here—she's accusing me of rape, of forcing her to have sex," Thornton said. "She went with me of her own free will, I swear it. You've got to help me, Aucielo. Someone's out to get me. I swear to God!"

Thornton was afraid the Cubans would lock him up and he'd never be heard from again. I told him that if they hadn't done so at this point, they probably wouldn't.

"Then why are those cops guarding me then?"

I went outside to talk to the policemen, but they would give me no information except that they would be with us on the trip back to Havana.

"Christina's death was bad publicity," Art said that night. "My guess is that after what you said to Castro, and to Guevara, the Cubans would like to see the last of us, and the sooner the better."

Before we left Santiago I had another conversation with Jake Campbell. I was too tired for any festivals. It was hot, and my door was open. When I realized Jake was standing in the doorway, I stopped working.

"I wanted to explain about Sharon," Campbell said. "Her story about Christina—she was just trying to calm the waters."

"But she did lie to me and then to the whole group."

"She didn't want to give any ammunition to the people who advocate invading Cuba. Sharon doesn't know what's going on. Neither do I. The Cubans don't seem to know. My guess is that the CIA or FBI or gusanos are trying to cause an international incident. Believe me, I—my party, I mean—doesn't benefit from this."

"You said before that Christina might've gotten mixed up in something. What were you thinking of?"

Campbell shook his head.

"Who are the agents in our group?"

"Can I come in?" He did, and closed the door. "I think Monica Chapman's an agent. And Frank Vara is definitely a gusano. And I think there might be a third person, but I don't know who, working for the FBI."

"Are you kidding about Monica?"

"Steve saw her taking pictures of Havana harbor. And those people you met with, the ones that set you up to ask Che those questions, she had contact with them too."

"Do you think Monica had something to do with Christina's death?"

Campbell had picked up on the disbelieving tone in my voice, and now the politician took over. He smiled. "No. I didn't say that. Look, we've just got a few more days in Cuba. Tomorrow we head back to Havana for the July 26th celebration. On the first or second of August we fly to Paris, then back to the States. I'm just asking you again to please hold up any stories about Christina's death, at least until we get home."

I nodded. In fact, I didn't plan to write anything about Christina until I knew more. I asked Campbell what he knew about the two cops and Dick Thornton.

"There was a previous accusation against him from somebody you'd think an unlikely victim, Helen Anderson. Now this American woman who lives in Havana, a translator for the Cuban Foreign Office in Havana, says Thornton invited her up to his room and raped her. The Cubans are very upset. They were ready to put him on a plane, but since we're leaving in a few days, I think they decided he's an American problem, not theirs. But they're keeping a close eye on him, and on the rest of us, until we leave."

"Could he have had anything to do with Christina?"

"Arlene now swears that Thornton was with her the night Christina died." Campbell shrugged. Both of us knew Thornton had publically accused her of being with someone else that night.

I told Monica about Jake Campbell's latest accusation.

"Do you think I'm a fink?" she asked.

"Of course not. But Campbell's saying you were photographing Havana Harbor."

"So what? You're not the only writer, Dante. I'd like to do an article on 'Life in Revolutionary Cuba.' I've been taking notes and pictures for it. Actually, almost everybody in the group's been taking pictures—of Havana Harbor, of the factories and schools we've visited, you name it."

She was right. As a group we must've taken hundreds if not thousands of photographs.

Stopping only for meals and one overnight stay in Santa Clara, we drove through to Havana in order to be back for the 26th of July celebration. On the bus, the complaints from Thornton became unbearable. To make matters worse, our best guide and translator, Maria, had stayed in Santiago. Ricardo said she had a boyfriend there. I wondered if Maria had just had all she could take of our group. The two Cuban cops who rode with us explained, in unconvincing English, that they were our new translators.

At the hotel in Santa Clara, I saw Helen sitting alone, and I took a seat next to her. I wanted to ask her about her incident with Thornton. We hadn't spoken much since I'd found her in my hotel room going through my articles, and when I sat next to her, she started to move. I stopped her by saying that in exchange for my cooperation in not writing about Christina Ward, I needed a little cooperation from the People's Revolutionary Party. Helen looked over to where Campbell was sitting, and she sat down again.

"What is it you want?" she said.

"Tell me what happened between you and the preacher."

"I was in his room—"

"Looking through his things."

She nodded. "And he came in, and forced me onto the bed. If Arlene hadn't come back, he would've raped me."

The next day we drove from Santa Clara back to Havana. It was July 24th, two days before the big celebration in honor of Castro's assault of the Moncada barracks. On the bus, Monica gave me a copy of his famous speech, "History Will Absolve Me."

27

As soon as we got back to the Havana Riviera Hotel, most of the group headed for the hotel pool. There were more guests in the lobby now, dignitaries who had come for the July 26th rally. Members of one group, from Southeast Asia, were dressed in black pajama-like clothes and wanted to talk to me about their struggles. I excused myself, saying I'd be glad to interview them later. Now, however, I was anxious to go through my photographs to see what Christina might have been looking for the night she'd vanished into my bathroom. So I went over to the Prensa office to retrieve the folders of contact prints and negatives and developed pictures I'd left there. Inside the newspaper office, half a dozen reporters from different countries were talking to each other. They'd all come for the July 26th celebration.

"What's new?" I asked Jose, the Cuban who managed the Prensa office.

"Let's see. The South Vietnamese want to attack the North. Castelo Bronco has extended his term as president of Brazil. There are riots in Singapore and New York. The price of sugar on the world market is falling. What's new with you? How was the trip?"

I nodded. "I'll have some articles and pictures for you tonight or tomorrow." I sat at his desk and looked over the international and national news reports. U.S. Marines at Guantanamo had fired again on Cuban sentries. Fidel's sister, who lived in Mexico, was denouncing him. The Venezuelan government charged Cuba with sponsoring guerrillas in its country. Regino Boti had been removed as Minister of the Economy. Cubans were again being urged to be vigilant. I wondered if this was the government's way to get people to spy on their neighbors. Then I remembered the pictures I'd been carrying around in my camera bag, the ones of some old man which I'd inadvertently picked-up from the Prensa office before leaving for the countryside. They were still there, in a pocket of my bag, and I handed them to Jose with my apologies.

"I hope these aren't important," I said. "I picked them up and took them out of here by mistake."

"Who is it?" Jose said.

I shrugged. "Like I said, I picked them up by mistake."

"These aren't mine. Looks like somebody's passport pictures. You know, the little photographs they glue into your passport."

"Nobody's missing these?"

"No one said anything to me."

My hotel room had been cleaned while we were touring the countryside. No doubt it had also been searched. I took the camera, the one with the timer, and loaded it with film. This was the camera that Christina had heard clicking. At the rally on the 26th, I would use it to get pictures of the speaker's platform while I took pictures from other places. But for now I set it up to find out if anyone besides Helen was coming into my room. I wished I'd had this camera working when somebody had tampered with the balcony railing. Now I set the timer and put it on the bureau in the living room. Then I took out all my negatives and contact prints and spread them on the bed. I didn't know what I was looking for, just something that would explain why Christina might have been interested in my pictures—if indeed she had been.

The shots featured members of the group, places we'd visited, Cuban officials, teachers, students, people I'd talked to and photographed at random, and of course several photos of Fidel Castro and Che Guevara. Already these pictures, which I'd taken so recently, had taken on a timeless quality. That was one of the things I liked about photography. But now, digging through all these pictures, I felt almost like I was drowning in them. If I'd somehow photographed something important, something Christina would have been interested in, I didn't have a clue what it could be. Now even the shots of her and Captain Fuentes looked innocuous. He was just a young man talking to a young woman. I had several of Christina next to Jake Campbell, and there were a few of Campbell with Maria Montalvo. She was a sweet girl, very pretty. Looking at photographs of her, I remembered I'd forgotten to write Felicia's sister, Mirta. I'd promised to write her and to send pictures.

Again I looked over the photos from our interview with Che Guevara: Captain Fuentes with a cigarette in his mouth, Captain Lima, who seemed to be dozing. Guevara leaning over his desk. Another one with his arms resting on the desk. A picture of Che leaning forward, his fingertips touching, eyebrows slightly raised. In another photo he was looking at one of the students who had asked a question. You couldn't help liking the face and trusting the man. He was a teacher, offering truths which he saw clearly and simply. For him, I thought, knowledge was for the common good—he was unlike Steve Bloomberg, who tried to use his little bit of knowledge about history to make himself superior. As Che had explained the Revolution, I'd felt included, part of a commonality. Certainly no other Cuban leader, including Fidel with his ping-pong paddle, had made me feel this way.

Another photo. Che gesturing to make a point, right hand raised. My notes said he was discussing moral versus material incentives. And in the next one he was talking about tin mines in Bolivia and latifundia in Peru and explaining how people were forced to live in hellish conditions. I remembered how Che had more than once glanced in my direction, suggesting to me that he was aware of my articles. There had been spontaneity in his responses to our questions, and compassion in his voice when he'd spoken of the poor.

As I looked at more photos, I wondered what Che had seen that had changed him from an ordinary but bright young man into a guerilla warrior. Probably, I thought, no more than was available to all of us— except that he identified with the victims. Did Jake Campbell and his comrades? I didn't think compassion was part of Jake Campbell's makeup, or Steve Bloomberg's. I hadn't felt it with Christina either. Then why were they revolutionaries? Felicia had been compassionate, perhaps too compassionate. I thought Monica Chapman was compassionate. What about the thousands of Americans who bought souvenirs and took pictures as they toured Latin America? Did they ever think about why the natives were so poor?

I spent the next two hours in my bathroom lab developing the new photos I'd taken. Then I went back through my contact prints. But I still couldn't find anything suspicious. And, unfortunately, many of my photographs didn't seem very good now.

After dinner, in the lobby, Richard Thornton approached me.

"What do you think of Cuba now?" he said.

I didn't want to get into a discussion with this man now, a man accused of raping or trying to rape at least two different women. I tried to walk away.

"I've had it with all this propaganda," Thornton said. "I know you've written a lot of favorable stuff about Cuba. Do you really believe in this crap? I didn't think you were one of Campbell's people."

"You're blocking my way."

"What do you think of them—the PRP?"

"They arranged this trip. I suppose I'm grateful for that."

"The newspaper you work for, the *Free Express*. Is it a commie paper? If you're not a member of Campbell's group, I'd say you're cheating him out of dues."

Getting away from Thornton, I suddenly felt exhausted by the trip around the countryside. I wanted to relax, and I headed for the jazz club near the hotel. But now it was crowded and noisy. After one drink I headed back to my room to sleep. The camera with the timer was where I'd set it on the mantle. I'd forgotten to turn the timer off. I checked the roll of film and decided it would be enough for the big rally.

As I went to sleep, a name Christina had mentioned—Dave Swan—popped into my head. I had asked Campbell about Swan, but he'd only told me the guy was dead. I made a mental note to ask him again.

28

At breakfast we learned that Campbell had scheduled us to meet a delegation of Vietnamese who were members of the National Liberation Front. These were the people in black pajama-like clothes whom I had seen the day before. They had set up a projector and were waiting for us in a room off the hotel lobby.

Although most members of the group were excited about the 26th of July celebrations the next day, and although none of us knew much about this Southeast Asian country we'd barely heard of, we were shocked by what we were now shown. The Vietnamese had been waging a war of national liberation against the French for years, and were now fighting the Americans. They were allied with their brothers and sisters in North Vietnam, but they insisted they were not Communists. Their goal, they said, was independence from foreign domination—Japanese, French, American, even Chinese. Their film gave a brief history of their struggle, and showed people fighting in jungles and shooting at soldiers who also looked Vietnamese. Then it showed pictures of people without legs or without arms or with horrible burn wounds. Felicia, I thought, would have taken up this new struggle as her own. I didn't really know how to respond. Was this war any of my business?

The film ended by quoting from the American Declaration of Independence.

"When you go home, tell your countrymen that we do not hate Americans," a young Vietnamese woman told us after the movie. "We respect America and your freedom and independence. This is what we treasure—to be independent and liberated, also with justice."

Did this woman really think anyone in the United States would listen to us about a country most Americans couldn't find on a map? I wondered if Mrs. Wilson would even print anything I wrote about Vietnam.

In the hotel lobby, I caught up with Helen Anderson. Since she'd talked to me in Santa Clara, I was hoping she might tell me something about Dave Swan.

"Dave Swan," I said. "Who was he?"

"David Swan? Why do you want to know about him?"

"Please, just tell me about him." The steel drum band was playing outside the hotel. Arriving guests flooded the lobby. We sat on the sofa where I'd been approached by the Cuban dissident, Adolfo.

"David was a warehouseman," Helen said. "He lived in Chicago. He was in the party. What else do you want to know?"

"What was his connection to Christina Ward?"

"A couple of years ago she was touring colleges in the Midwest, and he was assigned to drive her around. When she moved on to the Northeast, he followed her. He was married and had two kids. But he started showing up at campuses wherever she was speaking. He started wearing the beret Cuban guerrillas used to wear. He grew a beard and wore army fatigues. Then he moved with his family to New York, where Christina was." Helen seemed to drift away for a minute, then resumed. "David would sit next to her at meetings and sort of stare at her. His wife, Lucy, was at these meetings. It was embarrassing."

"Did Christina encourage him?"

"Not at all. When he started showing up at her apartment, she called Jake and some other comrades. But nobody could reason with David. Finally she called the police. That's when he tried to commit suicide."

I didn't know what to make of any of this. It didn't seem to have any relevance to what had happened to Christina.

"He tried," Helen continued, "but he failed—in the worst way. When he came out of the hospital, he was blind in one eye, half his face was paralyzed, and he dragged one leg. It was pathetic. He couldn't stop drool from rolling down his chin. His wife took him back to Chicago, but he immediately came back to New York and started following Christina again. One day he confronted her in the cafeteria at Columbia University. I happened to be with her that day, and I can tell you he made a terrible scene. He said all sorts of things—that she was leading him on and two-timing him, stuff like that. Crazy stuff that wasn't true. It was really scary.

We got away as quickly as we could. And that night David shot himself again. This time he was successful. He had a lovely wife and two lovely children."

It was raining again. I sat in a café drinking strong, sweet Cuban coffee, and listening to the rain on the pavement and the voices at the counter. Then the rain stopped. In a few moments the heat and humidity came back. Was there anything more to Christina's reference to Dave Swan than that she'd thought she was being followed? But we all were being followed.

I took a walk through the city. People were sweeping the streets in front of their stores and houses in preparation for tomorrow's celebration. I found myself walking along the Malecon, looking out at the water. When I got back to the hotel, Thornton was in the lobby arguing with Campbell. Apparently the preacher had been questioned by the police again. As I headed to the elevator, Thornton went on a tirade, calling the Cubans a bunch of racists. He said he'd never even talked to Maria Montalvo, and that the police should be questioning Campbell, who had talked to her every chance he got. I pressed the elevator button and waited. When the elevator arrived, several people got out, and by the time I entered, Thornton was alongside me. He swore softly to himself. I asked what he'd been saying about Maria.

"She took off with her boyfriend or something," Thornton said. "Only nobody can find her, so they start questioning the black man. It figures."

I got out of the elevator and walked slowly to my room. Thornton was right about Campbell, who'd been sniffing around Maria. Campbell had been close to Christina, and at one time he'd been close to Felicia. There was music coming from a street near the hotel, and music coming from the steel drum band in front of the hotel. Two young women were dead. But there was something else, another piece. What was it? Christina, for her own purposes—whatever they were—had flirted with men, perhaps with Dave Swan, perhaps with Captain Fuentes. And she'd flirted with me. But Maria Montalvo definitely had not. And now she'd disappeared. When we'd been told she wasn't coming back to Havana with us but would instead be staying in Santiago with her boyfriend, I'd thought it strange because Maria was such a dedicated person. I'd assumed she'd simply been replaced by those plainclothes cops who hardly spoke English and who wanted to keep an eye on Thornton because of the rape allegations. Then I remembered Anne Montrose, also a dedicated person, who had suddenly dropped out of the Cuba trip. In New York, Anne had telephoned and asked me to meet her at the museum, but she'd never shown up.

I went into my room, took out my photographs, and started digging through them one more time.

This time I found something I hadn't seen before. In the first batch of prints there was a picture of Christina. I placed it next to a photo of Maria. Then from my wallet I took out the photo of Felicia. And because it was right in front of me, I place a fourth photo next to the other three. This was a picture I'd taken of Anne Montrose outside a restaurant somewhere in the Midwest.

"What's up?" Campbell was buttoning his shirt, getting ready, I guessed, to go out on the town.

"Jake, what did Anne Montrose say to you about dropping out of this trip?"

"Anne?" He stopped the buttoning. "What do you want to know about her for? Anyway I didn't talk to her. Her boyfriend called."

I didn't know what to believe from this man who made a career of lying, who probably lied just out of habit.

"Who was it, Jake? Do you remember the boyfriend's name?"

"I don't know. I don't remember. What's going on?"

"Do you know what happened to Maria?"

"She supposedly stayed with a boyfriend in Santiago, but who knows? Why did you ask me about Anne Montrose? What's she got to do with Maria?"

As I took the elevator to the lobby, I remembered the policeman in San Francisco, Detective Mantz, who had ignored my theories about gusanos and political conspiracies. Wanting to talk to Ricardo, I went to the ECAP office, the bureau for tourism and friendship, but our guide wasn't there. A man named Manuel was the only one around. I asked him about Maria Montalvo, but he got defensive. Why did I want to know about Maria?

"Do you know if there was anyone in our group that she was especially friendly with?" I said.

"What business is that of yours?"

"I need to know."

"Write about our new housing and our new schools. That is what you are here for."

Manuel wouldn't give me Ricardo's address or tell me how to reach him by phone. I went out to the lobby. First I called the Prensa office. Jose Zambala wasn't there. Who could I ask for help in Cuba? I tried to reach Captain Lima, Che Guevara's assistant, who had visited me at the hotel. It was impossible to reach him. It took me almost an hour to get through to the *Free Express* in Berkeley, California. When I finally did, I told Mrs. Wilson what I needed and that I'd hold while she made calls on another line. She said the information better be worth the cost of this phone bill. Ten minutes later, she said she'd have to get back to me.

"It's Saturday, Dante. Nobody's around. And it's already night in New York."

"We're leaving in a few days. Try to get back to me as soon as you can."

My only contact in New York was Charley Jessup. I prayed he'd be in, and got hold of him just as he was leaving his apartment.

"It's the weekend, buddy. I probably won't be able to do anything until Monday."

I told Charley how to reach me.

"It's important," I said.

I needed to talk to somebody, so I tried Art Sparrow. Then I tried Monica, but she wasn't around either. Probably, like the rest of our group, they were out on the town partying on this eve of the July 26th celebrations. Frustrated, I went out on my balcony and checked the railing, which had been repaired. I looked out at the sea. The lights on the Florida Straits probably belonged to the U.S.S. *Oxford*, which likely was cruising back and forth to enforce the embargo. Eighteen floors below me, Christina Ward had drowned. I went inside to look at my photos again.

Photographs. I'd become fascinated with taking pictures when I was eight years old and had gotten lost on my way home from the Parkside Theater. I'd gone to see a movie, *Wake of the Red Witch*, which was about finding lost treasure, but it hadn't been shown at the Children's Matinee. I remembered that leaving the theater, I'd been shocked. Night had fallen. The neighborhood I knew by day was transformed. Streets and houses I knew by daylight had turned nightmarish. I remembered how, hoping I would recognize somebody, I had run close to one house and peeked through the front window. Then I had looked in the front windows of every house along the street, and as I did so, each window became a frame, and the life inside became only another picture, and my fear subsided. No matter how frightening something was, I could turn it into a picture.

Now the opposite was happening. Simple photographs were turning into nightmares. As I studied the photographs I'd taken of four different women, the resemblance between them was undeniable. How could I have missed it? Each woman was small, each was pretty, each had a dark complexion. What was not in the photographs was my knowledge that each woman had been political. Was this all just coincidence? Two of them were dead, one was missing, and the other, Anne Montrose—I didn't know. I tried reaching Captain Lima again, and left a message.

29

For the July 26th celebration, our group, including the two policemen who were now accompanying us everywhere, were seated with other guests of honor just below the platform where Fidel would speak. By the time we arrived, the Plaza of the Revolution was already packed with thousands of people, many of them carrying rifles.

"There's your democracy," Campbell said to us. "An armed citizenry. Any one of these people could kill Castro if they wanted."

"I prefer the secret ballot and open elections," Monica said.

I placed the camera with the timer on a tripod, focused it on the microphone Castro would speak into, and asked Monica to keep an eye on it. Then, taking my other two cameras and slinging a bag of film around my neck, I set out to wander through the crowd and document the event. I wanted close-ups of ordinary Cubans as they listened to their leader.

I'd never before seen a crowd of over a million people. If this estimate was correct, that was about a sixth of the Cuban population. The entire Plaza was filled, and people filled the surrounding streets as well. Banners depicting heroes and martyrs like Camillo Clenfuegos waved above us.

Fidel spoke for over four hours. He attacked the United States, and time after time brought thousands of campesinos to an emotional climax by expressing support for other struggles against American imperialism. I used up my film before he finished, and since his entire speech would be published, I went back to the hotel. I wanted to develop my best shots, write my story, and send everything off as soon as possible. I knew the Prensa office would be crowded with the reporters from all over, so I wanted to get there first.

Mrs. Wilson would want pictures of Fidel speaking, so I began with these. When I got to the roll of film from the stationary camera, the first pictures were of my hotel room, taken from the mantle where I'd placed the camera and had forgotten to turn it off. It was one of these shots, snapped before the timer camera began taking pictures of the speaker's platform at today's rally, which stopped me cold. Unlike the other photos of my empty hotel room, this photo had captured a person's back. The person was not me. I reached for the magnifying glass. Only part of the back showed at the left edge of the picture, but I knew immediately who it was. I went out to the balcony and checked the railing, but it seemed solid. I looked through the rest of my suite, but could find nothing unusual.

I had to wait until the rally was over and the group returned to the hotel. In the meantime, I continued developing film and selecting pictures to send to Mrs. Wilson. Finally I heard American voices drifting up from the swimming pool. Taking one picture with me, the photo of the person's back, I went to Art Sparrow's room. He wasn't there. I asked at the pool, but nobody had seen him. Even Thornton was in the pool today, standing waist deep at the shallow end. The two Cuban policemen were sitting under an umbrella, drinking Cokes. I looked around the lobby. Frank Vara was playing chess with a female soldier. Arlene Washington sat by herself. I went back to my room, finished my article on the rally, and took it, along with my best photos, to the Prensa office. I still hadn't finished the articles I was writing about the countryside, but they could wait.

After dropping off my story and photos with Jose, I headed back to the hotel. On the way, I stopped at a street stand and had a strong coffee. People were talking and shouting. The excitement was building for the parties which would go on all night.

As I watched the street scene, I wondered again how I'd picked up those photos Jose still said were not his. If they hadn't come from his office, where had they come from? Then I thought about betrayals. Somebody pretends to be your friend but isn't. I remembered an incident in high school. Wayne something-or-other. After swearing a friend to secrecy, Wayne, needing to share his secret with somebody, had confessed to homosexual feelings. But the friend he confided in blabbed Wayne's secret to their other friends, and like wildfire it had spread through the school. Wayne and his family had moved away over the summer. But his friend—now I remembered that the friend's name was Dan—had continued at school, and I'd had classes with him. And looking at him in class, I'd wondered how he'd felt about betraying the boy who confided in him.

Art Sparrow, overweight, hairy but muscular, was wearing a pair of shorts but no shoes or socks or shirt when he answered his door. He invited me inside and poured me a drink.

"I've been expecting you," Art said. "Have you heard? We're leaving tomorrow."

"Tomorrow?"

"I guess the Cubans want us out of here."

"What were you doing in my room, Art?"

Sparrow held out a glass of rum. The chess board was set up with a game we'd been playing on the bus.

"I think I've got you this time," he said.

"I almost fell eighteen stories when the railing of my balcony gave way. If I find out you did that—and I don't care if you're FBI or CIA or what—I'm going to hang you off your own balcony so you know how it feels."

"I didn't have anything to do with that. Honestly, it upset me too."

I didn't really think he was responsible for the railing, but I wanted him to know I was angry. "So what were you doing in my room?" I said. "What were you looking for?"

This man, whom I'd asked to be my lawyer in San Francisco, this man I'd thought was a friend, put his forefinger to his lips and glanced around. "Not now," he said. "Not here. We'll talk later. I'll take you to dinner in Paris. I know some wonderful restaurants there. But we can't talk now."

"I saw you at civil rights demonstrations in Berkeley. Were you just there to take names and report on the demonstrators?"

"Listen—"

"When you 'helped' me with the police in San Francisco, did you and the cops have a few good laughs behind my back?"

"Let's finish our game of chess."

"Do you know what Lenin said about chess?"

"I didn't know you were a fan of Lenin's."

"He said it's too serious to be a game, and too much of a game to be taken seriously." Looking at Art Sparrow, I wondered if he was any worse, or any different, from Christina or Frank Vara. They were probably on different sides—I still didn't know all the players and the teams—but their game was the same. Spying. Betrayal.

"What about this? After each move, we'll each take a drink of rum."

"I read the book, and I saw the movie. You didn't answer my question. Why were you in my room?"

He lit his pipe. "We'll talk. I promise. But you have to wait." He glanced around. "We can't talk here. The walls have ears."

I looked at the chess pieces, and reached out to move a pawn. That's what I was, I thought, just a pawn.

"Mate in two moves," I said, and left.

Back in my room I looked again at the picture the camera had taken of Art Sparrow's back. It was a poor picture. The figure was leaning over as if looking for something. He was not at the desk, where I'd seen Helen Anderson reading my articles. He seemed to be lifting the cushion on a chair. I went over to the same chair and examined it. Of course, given the way I'd placed the camera, there would be no shots of him, or of anybody else, in other parts of this room or in the bedroom or in the bathroom where I developed my negatives and stored all my pictures.

"The bathroom," I said aloud, "where I develop negatives and store my photos." The bathroom… where Christina had gone the last time she'd come to my room. I took out all my photos and contact prints once again. This time I spread them across the floor. They were pretty much in chronological order so that they would match the notes I had in my notebooks. Now I rearranged them, putting all the photos of Christina, Maria, and Anne in a separate stack. Then I began categorizing everything else, not by date but by subject.

When I finished I still had a few pictures left over. These were the pictures of the old man. They weren't mine. Nor were they Jose Zambala's. According to Jose, nobody had been asking for them at the Prensa office.

So whose were they? If they hadn't come from the Prensa office, how had I gotten them? I got my magnifying glass and looked at them closely. Just photos of an old man. But studying them through the magnifying glass, I noticed something familiar about this particular old man. I got out one of the books Monica had loaned me and turned the pages until I found what I was looking for. Then I made comparisons. Satisfied, I telephoned Captain Lima. This time I got through to Che Guevara's assistant.

Lima was waiting for me in the lobby, talking to our guide, Ricardo. He indicated I should follow him into the ECAP office, and asked Ricardo to give us privacy.

Lima looked older now. Before, I hadn't noticed how much gray was in his hair or how lined his face was.

I said, "I want to know about Maria Montalvo."

He said, "Unfortunately we don't have all the facts."

"What facts do you have?"

"Maria Montalvo did not stay with her boyfriend in Santiago. She drowned. The authorities in Santiago recovered her body and believed that she was one of those who try to leave Cuba illegally. Perhaps heading for Haiti, although that is not usually where people go. But the medical examination determined the girl suffered—"

"An injury?" I said. "A broken neck?"

Lima stared at me. Finally he nodded. "We do not know if this was the work of an exile group or CIA agents or who was involved. Of course, our investigation continues. But your group is scheduled to leave Cuba tomorrow. That is earlier than previously planned, but it must be. For us to detain United States citizens is impossible. Due to the state of relations between our two countries, Cuba cannot appear to be holding United States citizens hostage, especially if we do not know who to arrest and do not have sufficient evidence."

"You've been following us everywhere since we arrived. Surely you must have some idea."

"But we have not been following any of you! Cuba has allowed you complete freedom to travel as you please."

Maybe Lima was telling the truth. Maybe some Cuban agency he didn't work with had been searching our rooms and following us. I said,

"I'm wondering if there are any other missing women, women who will turn up drowned. Our group has been all over the island. Have we been leaving a trail of drowned bodies behind us?"

Lima stepped back in shock.

"With their necks broken," I added.

Recovering himself, the captain said, "You mentioned some photographs on the telephone. May I see them?"

I took out the photos and handed them over.

"May I ask where you got these?"

"They turned up with my other photographs. I thought I'd picked them up by mistake at the Prensa office, but now I don't think so. I think somebody put them in with my other photos. I think the idea was that they would be mixed in with the hundreds of other pictures I've taken in Cuba."

There was a knock, and Lima indicated I should let him answer it. I couldn't see who was outside— I only heard some talking in Spanish. Then Lima and the other person came inside the ECAP office.

The other person was Commandante Ernesto 'Che' Guevara.

30

The next morning I had two telephone messages from the United States. The first was from Charley Jessup—so far nothing on the whereabouts of Anne Montrose. The other was from Mrs. Wilson, who said that the Montrose family assumed that their daughter was still in New York, but that they hadn't heard from her in weeks.

Worried that the books and pamphlets they'd collected in Cuba would be confiscated by U.S. Customs, people were busy packing these things to mail home. Before going to the Jose Marti Airport, we had breakfast with our official hosts, a delegation from the Federation of University Students. Frank Vara was missing. Ricardo, the guide, explained that Vara had taken a job here in Cuba. Because Vara had pulled me to safety, I took this to mean he was a Cuban agent and not a gusano, but of course it might have meant the opposite. Art Sparrow ate by himself and didn't look at me.

As we loaded our suitcases onto the bus, it was obvious that most of the group were anxious to go home, and were glad to be hustled off to the airport. On the bus trip to the airport, I stared lackadaisically at the gigantic billboards with revolutionary slogans, but by now I was so used to them they made no impression. I was thinking again about the man Christina Ward had mentioned—Dave Swan. She'd met Swan in the context of politics, but his obsession with her hadn't been political. It had been extremely irrational. I'd been wrong, looking for political plots, for conspiracies, for evil machinations on the part of Cuban exiles or the People's Revolutionary Party or the FBI or Soviet or East European spies. There were certainly FBI and CIA plots—Art Sparrow was proof of that—and no doubt People's Revolutionary Party plots, and Cuban counter-revolutionary plots, and plots from Adolfo's dissident group, and plots reaching into Che Guevara's office. Plots and counter-plots, and all of them rational, at least from the points of view of the plotters.

But Felicia, Christina, and Maria—and possibly Anne Montrose—had not been killed for a political reason. Their "crime" was that they were young and pretty, with similar physical features, and they had been involved in a political arena which permitted them to come into contact with the irrational, with a madman like David Swan, who had stalked Christina but had killed himself instead of her. Their deaths didn't have anything to do with logic or politics. They were victims of somebody's dark impulses, impulses triggered by something—some deeply buried thing which had suddenly been freed—motives I hadn't seen because I'd had the wrong chess board in my mind. I'd been digging for clues in all the wrong places. The Cubans couldn't help me. They had their own problems, and they were relieved to see the last of us. I was alone, and I was afraid, like when I was a kid and found myself stranded in that vast expanse of water, waiting for the tide to come in and drown me. I sat with Monica and told her about Maria Montalvo. For the first time, Monica was speechless. I then told her I believed Maria's and Christina's and Felicia's killer was amongst us. I didn't think she was in danger, but still warned her to be careful.

When we touched down in Bermuda for refueling, Art Sparrow waved for me to follow him to the airport bar. He ordered us each a beer.

"I'm going to tell you a few things because I like you," he said. Campbell and Helen Anderson were talking at the other end of the bar. Monica was waiting for me a few stools away. Then a few others from the group came in. Sparrow took our beers and moved to a table.

"First off," he said, "You should reconsider our offer. I'd heard you were sharp. I'd say you're a natural—that timer on your camera." He laughed.

"What were you looking for in my room?"

"Something that doesn't belong to you and that you wouldn't be interested in, and if you were, it would only cause you problems. By the way, I heard your camera click, but I left the film in it because I knew you'd see it and want to talk to me. Anyway, the Cubans got to your photos before I did. They're good."

"Do you know who killed Christina—and Felicia Vasquez and Maria Montalvo?"

"Maria?" He lowered his voice. "I certainly didn't have anything to do with any of that. I was watching Christina Ward, which was certainly not her real name. The reason I went into your hotel room was because you told me that Christina been to your room twice, the last time just before she was killed. You thought she was looking for something. I thought that she wasn't looking for something but was instead leaving something in your room, which would be a perfect place to hide what she had." He took out the same photographs of the old man which I'd handed over to Captain Lima, the photographs I'd assumed had been accidently picked up from the Prensa office.

Sparrow continued. "They're obsolete now, of course. As soon as the Cubans learned they were out in the world, they became useless." He looked at the photos. "Good make-up artists, don't you think? It's so they can travel unrecognized. Look at the facial structure, especially the very pronounced brow. Look closely."

I nodded. I'd seen the same things when I'd looked at these photos with a magnifying glass and compared them to photos of Che Guevara in a book Monica had loaned me.

"I'm not positive. We know he's trying to launch something in Africa or Latin America. They've been training guerrillas. We know that. They know we know it. Innocent people are going to die, Aucielo. Argentinean, Mexican, maybe Chilean or South African—in all likelihood mostly students, kids your age or younger. Kids with rifles and some ammunition who will volunteer to go into the hills outside Caracas or wherever and start their own guerrilla wars. The military in Latin American and African countries are not romantic. It's not a Hollywood production to them. These kids will be slaughtered. Guevara's guerrilla nonsense is deadly." Sparrow sipped his beer. "Christina got these pictures from the man you met in the lobby of the Havana Riviera before our interview with Guevara. Adolfo—that's what he was calling himself. He infiltrated a group of Cuban dissidents affiliated with a Latin American group founded by a guy named Juan Posadas. She wasn't working directly with Adolfo. There had to be some intermediary. For a while I thought it might be you. It's possible she was East German, Stasi. Maybe she was Russian. We know a few things about her. She operated in the States. At one time she tried to pass herself off as a counter-revolutionary Cuban, like your friend Frank Vara, who's definitely Cuban intelligence."

"Is this why she was killed? These photos?"

"Yes." Sparrow looked at me. When I'd first met him in Berkeley, he'd reminded me of a big teddy bear. He didn't look much like a teddy bear now.

"What about Felicia Vasquez?"

"What about her?"

"She was killed the same way Christina was. And probably Maria Montalvo. And maybe a woman named Anne Montrose." Sparrow was looking across the room. "Their deaths didn't have anything to do with photographs or guerrillas or spies. There's a maniac in this group, Art Sparrow, or whatever your real name is. A killer. A madman."

This man who had pretended to be my friend set his glass on the table and pushed his chair back. "I don't know what Felicia Vasquez's story was. Maybe that was a sex crime. I'm told she'd had sex before she was killed."

"Her neck was broken," I said. "Like Christina's."

"That doesn't mean much. It's probably a common m.o. It could be that the same person was responsible. It could be a ruse, kind of a copycat thing, but with different motives. I don't know. I'd look first at the Cubans. I don't know why Vara or one of his associates would kill Vasquez, but they had reasons to be after Ward, and might very well try to disguise her death in order not to provoke an ally."

"What about Maria and Anne Montrose?"

"Anne Montrose was one of the people who stayed in New York. I assume she thought twice about this trip and decided she didn't want to jeopardize her law career. I don't know what this Cuban girl was involved in."

"These murders didn't have anything to do with politics," I said. I tried to explain that they were about a different kind of insanity, but Sparrow had his own system, a grid which he laid over the chaos to make sense out of things, and like Jake Campbell, and perhaps the Cubans, and certainly me until a few hours earlier, he wasn't prepared to deal with anything that didn't fit the logic of his own chess board, which for him was the Cold War, spies, and power.

I followed Sparrow's gaze and saw Dr. Marcus, the agent who had tried to recruit me in San Francisco, standing in a doorway at the other end of the bar, flanked by British policemen in white shirts and navy-blue shorts.

"That photograph of the old man," I said. "I gave the other copies to Captain Lima. You remember Captain Lima, Che Guevara's assistant?"

"It doesn't matter. You make your choices. By the way, do you know what's waiting for you back home? It's not just your passport or a fine or maybe jail. It's your career." He drained his beer and wiped his mouth with the back of his hand. "Let's say you're lucky and you find a decent job. You're working for one, two weeks. Then one day the boss calls you to his office, hands you a final paycheck and smiles. No explanation. You don't know why you've been fired, and you're never going to know for sure. But there it is. Every time, every decent job. Of course, you can work for Mary Wilson or somebody like her for the next twenty years."

"Doesn't it matter to you that there's a madman on the loose killing young women?"

"Detective Mantz in San Francisco has you down as his number one suspect, Aucielo. Did you know that? Some of the stuff they released to the papers about Clifton Specks—that was actually about you. And Anne Montrose—if something has happened to her, you would be a prime suspect, wouldn't you? Didn't you drive across the country with her? Of course, you were flirting with Christina Ward. And Maria Montalvo—you knew her too, didn't you?" Sparrow stepped away from the table. "I'd say you have a lot of explaining to do when you get home. Now I've got another plane to catch. Oh, by the way, I move my rook to queen's bishop two."

"Pawn takes knight," I said, and watched him walk away from me and towards his colleague, Dr. Marcus, and the British policemen. Then he disappeared.

The rest of the group, arguing about who had suspected Art Sparrow earliest, flew on to Paris. And as we crossed the Atlantic for the third time, I wondered if the person who had killed at least three women was still among us. I thought about Christina, who had flirted with me and hid her photos amongst the hundreds I'd taken. If she hadn't been killed, I'd never have noticed them. I would have taken them home along with the rest of my pictures, unless the Cubans found them first and arrested me. Was this why she'd recruited me for the trip—to help her smuggle something out of Cuba? Without realizing what the pictures were, or might be, I'd found them and put them in my camera bag to give to Jose Zambala at the Prensa office. But was Sparrow telling the truth about her? I had no idea. I looked at my fellow travelers. Was one of them the carrier of a deadly plague? Dick Thornton, the ex-preacher and Black Nationalist? He might be a sexual predator, but was he also a murderer? Jake Campbell? He'd known all four women. Politics and power, not sex, seemed uppermost for him. Perhaps BJ Johnson, the All-American former student body president from Berkeley. He'd known all four. Or could it be Steve Bloomberg, who dressed like a worker from the thirties and quoted Lenin? Maybe Sparrow was right, and it was Frank Vara, who was still in Cuba. Or was I looking in the wrong place? Perhaps the killer was a woman. I wondered if I'd missed something else in my photos. I needed to go through them again. I hadn't been observing closely enough. I'd missed things. I'd missed too much.

I asked Monica, "Could anyone have known in 1917 that a stalwart Bolshevik like Stalin would turn out to be a mass murderer?"

"What?"

"Is there any way to tell what evils Fidel Castro or even Che Guevara might commit in the future?"

She waited for me to finish my thought.

"Chaos," I said. "Not logic. Not rational, conscious planning. The irrational, buried deep in the human personality. That's what determines the fates of millions."

"Maybe that other German Jew, Freud and not Marx, was right after all," she said, "and until we find a way to change ourselves, revolutions will merely be a matter of rearranging the same old furniture."

In which case, I thought, Che Guevara's moral incentives and his project of creating 'socialist man' were just more utopian dreams.

Thinking about Felicia in her bathtub and Christina in the hotel swimming pool and Maria in the Caribbean and maybe Anne Montrose in the Hudson or the East River—three and possibly four murders—I walked up and down the aisle of the plane, completely distracted. When Monica asked if I was feeling all right, I wondered if she had been saved by her height and complexion, and if Helen Anderson had been saved by being overweight, and Arlene Washington by being black. Sharon Albright, unlike the victims I knew about, was not all that bright, but she was the one woman in the group, and on the plane now, who fit the profile—petite, rather delicate, certainly attractive, and sympathetic to revolution. I stopped and looked at her. She was sitting between BJ and Jake Campbell. And she'd been to my room too. For a moment I had a paranoid thought. Maybe the killer was in some way focusing on me. But I'd hardly known Maria, and had only sat next to Anne Montrose on the car trip. I took my seat again and looked at Sharon. I wanted to sit next to her, to talk to her, but she talking to Campbell. Now BJ was showing her something. When several members of the group had given speeches at a Mothers of Martyrs rally, it had been BJ's speech and picture which had made the newspaper and television. When we played ping-pong with Fidel, again it had been BJ who got in the newspapers. He was photogenic, tall, handsome, athletic, a great smile. The all-American boy. Everybody liked him. The only person BJ himself hadn't liked had been Clifton Specks because Specks didn't wash and smelled bad. But even Clifton had liked BJ.

I found myself concentrating on BJ Johnson, trying to remember how he'd related to Anne Montrose on our car trip, and what he'd said about Felicia.

And then there was Jacob Campbell. And Steve Bloomberg.

When Sharon got up to go to the toilet, I followed her.

"What will you do when you get home?" she asked me.

"Maybe travel. My boss has sold some of my stories and pictures, so I'll have a little money. I'd like to see more of Latin America."

"I'm going to work with the Student Committee to Uphold the Right to Travel. We're calling it SCURT. Jake wants us to tour the colleges. You could help. Could I use some of your pictures for a slide show?"

I nodded. Then I said, "You and BJ have become pretty friendly."

"He's thinking about joining the Peace Corps and going to Africa. It's something I've considered. But I don't know." She started talking about being Catholic and being a Communist. I wasn't really following her, because I was watching BJ and Campbell. Campbell was smiling.

We stopped for fuel at the Canary Islands, then headed to Madrid. From Madrid we caught a connecting flight to Paris.

As we were leaving the plane at Orly Airport to enter Paris for the second time, I watched Sharon and thought about her resemblances to the other victims, and I wondered if her scatterbrained conversation had saved her. She was ahead of me on the stairway, which had been wheeled to the plane so that passengers could climb down to the tarmac and go into the terminal building. Reporters were waiting on the ground and flashing pictures as we came out of the plane. There was one person walking between Sharon and me. When Sharon reached the ground, she smiled at a photographer and started walking through the crowd of reporters towards the terminal. The person between her and me paused on the second or third step and looked around. He was smiling. I thought that he was also glad to be back. Maybe he was looking forward to a day or two in Paris before we flew home. Then he jumped, or sort of hopped, to the ground. It was a happy gesture, that little hop. It said, 'Glad to be back in the Free World,' or 'Glad to be in France.' But in my mind, I saw something else. I saw a stairway on Precita Avenue in San Francisco, the stairway which led from Felicia Vasquez's apartment to the street, the stairway her landlord, old man Broussard, had said he'd heard somebody come down the night Felicia was killed. Broussard had said the person jumped the last two or three steps to the street. Just as BJ Johnson had now jumped the last two or three steps from the airplane to the ground. Billy "BJ" Johnson. William Johnson. The former student body president of the University of California. The handsome, friendly boy-man who had appeared on Cuban television more than anyone else in the group because everyone loved him. Now he'd caught up with Sharon and was walking with her into the airport building.

31

I called Mrs. Wilson in Berkeley from our hotel in Paris. She told me that Anne Montrose was assumed to be still in New York. Charley Jessup had been unable to learn anything at all about Anne from the New York police. To make sure nothing happened to Monica, I insisted we share a room. Our hotel was on the Boulevard Voltaire. Once again I got out my photos and spread them on the bed.

"Because he jumped down two or three steps?" Monica said. "You're the one who's making a leap."

"Look at these." In the contact sheets I found pictures of BJ next to Christina and Maria, and also behind both women at various times, and in two of the photos he seemed to be staring at Christina. I knew these pictures weren't proof of anything, no more than the little jump down the stairs that I'd seen at the airport. Monica sat on the one chair in the room and looked at me as if I were crazy.

In my notebook I found what BJ had told me about his background. His parents, he said, were socialites who had become socialists in the thirties. His father, William Johnson, Sr., had become a labor organizer and had met BJ's mother at a peace rally at the University of Chicago. They had been active in various progressive organizations in the forties, but had withdrawn from politics during the McCarthy witchhunts of the fifties. BJ, born during World War Two, had a sister, Lindsey, born after the war. He said his uncle, Lawrence Johnson, had been living in China for several years.

I left Monica in the room and went looking for Johnson, who was sharing a room with Steve Bloomberg. I knocked. No one answered. I knocked again, and then, for an instant, remembered knocking at Felicia's door on Precita Avenue. I tried the door handle. It didn't turn, but the key to my room worked for this room also. Opening the door, I called out, then went inside and closed the door. I knew BJ's luggage from our drive across the country. His suitcase and knapsack were at the foot of one of the beds. I opened the suitcase. In a rush, I dumped everything onto the floor. After I'd emptied the knapsack also, which contained mostly dirty laundry, I went back to the suitcase. But I could find nothing incriminating. I stuffed everything back, and left the room. My hope—that I might find something belonging to either Christina or Maria in BJ's suitcase—had gone unsatisfied. I went down to the lobby. BJ was there, waiting for Sharon. Monica had also come downstairs.

"I need to talk to you," I said to the man I was certain had murdered Felicia and the others.

BJ, looking through a New York Herald Tribune, turned and smiled at me.

"I just had a phone call from San Francisco," I said. I was standing over him.

"Everything okay?"

"Not quite. Felicia Vasquez's landlord has identified you as the person he saw leaving her apartment the night she was killed."

BJ laughed. "Is this your idea of a joke?" he said. He looked over at Monica.

"Why were you at her apartment that night?" I said.

Johnson stood up. He was taller than I was, and much more athletic. "Are you accusing me of something?" he said. He wasn't smiling now. "Are you trying to say I had something to do with your girlfriend's death?" He took a step towards me so that he was only inches away. "She was my friend, too, you know." If he'd stopped there, I wouldn't have known what to do. It had been a stupid bluff, made out of frustration. But he continued. He was so close I could feel his breath on my face. "The police questioned me. Did you know that? They weren't really interested in me, but they asked about you. They wanted to know if you'd ever shown me any pornographic pictures. They said you took dirty pictures of her. I was shocked, Aucielo—shocked that Felicia would've posed for such things. Your friend's into dirty pictures," he said, looking over at Monica. "You never know about people, do you?"

What photographs was he talking about? He saw my confusion. He saw my weakness, and he couldn't stop himself. "Naturally I can't remember which nights I spent with that hot tamale. I guess there were several." He smiled. I hadn't seen this side of Johnson before. I thought probably nobody had, except for his victims. He was enjoying himself. "One thing I do remember," he continued, as if unable to stop himself. "Yeah. She thought you were an asshole. Of course, a lot of people think you're an asshole. I guess I do too. You have to excuse me now. I have a date."

"With Sharon?"

"She thinks you're an asshole too."

He was too confident. He'd shown me just enough cruelty to convince me, in spite of my lack of real evidence, that I was right. I wanted to hit him. I wanted to smash the heel of my hand into the bottom of his nose and drive the bone into his brain. I wanted to watch the blood gush out of his smiling face. It's an easy punch. I had only to bring my arm up quickly. My palm wouldn't need to land squarely or with much force. It would sting like hell and blind him. Then, while he was blinded, I'd proceed to tear him apart.

Sharon came into the lobby with Steve Bloomberg, and without another glance BJ walked away. I wanted to tell Sharon what I thought and that she should be careful. But I knew my suspicions were too vague, and at this point unprovable. Besides, she liked BJ. She was obviously flattered by his attentions. Yes, everybody liked him.

The three of them were talking on the other side of the lobby. I was standing with Monica. Then Sharon came over to me.

"You used me in Havana," she said. "And now you want to use me again—is that what this is about? I felt bad for you after Christina's accident. Because of her, a lot of us excused your outbursts in front of Che and Fidel. I don't know what you're trying to do, Dante. What do you want from BJ? He's somebody everybody likes. The Cubans loved him. I've never heard anyone ever say anything bad about him until this. It's a horrible thing to say."

Sharon and BJ left the hotel together. The last thing I heard Johnson say was that I had better stop spreading "bullshit nonsense" about him, or he was going to "clean my clock."

I thought, I'll be with you, Johnson, wherever you go. And I'll have my camera.

Because the Cubans had speeded up our departure, we had two days in Paris before our flight to New York. I again tried to make contact with Mike Pettit, my friend who was studying in Paris. Having lived here for a year, he might be able to help me.

"I got your postcard from Cuba," Pettit said over the telephone. "Sorry I missed you last time. But listen, Dante, after you were here last month, I've been followed all over the place. Wherever I go, it seems there's somebody behind me—often wearing a trench coat! Listen, I'm sorry, but I'm not sure it's a good idea for us to see each other right now. I need to renew my student visa."

I asked Monica, who was the only one in the group who didn't think I was completely insane, to help me. That night she and I followed BJ and Sharon to a restaurant, and then back to the hotel. Exhausted, I sat for a long time soaking in the hotel bathtub.

From the other room, Monica was talking to me.

I called back, "The disregard of another life, the viciousness of a killer, how do you understand it?" The hot water relaxed my body, but my mind wouldn't stop spinning the same questions around and around. Was a murderer like Johnson something that came out of the same society which lynched black people? I remembered Arlene Washington's story about her father. How do you eliminate hatred?

Monica said something I couldn't hear through the closed door. My thoughts continued to spin. I couldn't stop myself. We came, all of us, from a society based on egoism and selfishness. But was irrationality a permanent feature of our species, impervious to all utopian schemes like Che Guevara's? Monica opened the bathroom door and stared at me from the doorway.

"You're talking to yourself, Dante. Are you okay?"

"How do we stop him from killing again?"

With Monica staring at me, I climbed out of the tub, dried off, and flopped on the bed. I was so tired I thought I'd be asleep as soon as my head hit the pillow. But I couldn't sleep. I got up and dug through my photos again. How many times had I gone through them? I wondered how many other people had also been going through them.

In the morning, while Sharon and BJ were still sleeping, I took a taxi to the American Embassy, where a young secretary listened to me as if I were insane. Very courteously, he said that "suspicions of a crime are not evidence," and that if I wanted to wait, I could talk to another official. After half an hour I was ushered into the office of a man named Hightower, who nodded and identified me as "the reporter whose pro-Cuba stories were an embarrassment to our country."

"I know all about you, Mr. Aucielo," Hightower said, mispronouncing my name. He had long hair which seemed styled, and a purplish nose.

"Not oh-see-el-o. My name rhymes with cello."

"You have a vendetta against your own country. You're a troublemaker. But I must say this is a unique way to make trouble."

Seeing that I wasn't going to get any help from this quarter, I headed for the French police. A light rain was falling. Between the American Embassy, which was near the Place de la Concorde, and the main police station, which was several confusing blocks away, I was sure I was being followed. I walked down Rue de Rivoli, alongside a park and not far from the river. I stopped for coffee at a stand up bar and ate a croissant on the street. I slowed down, turned a corner, stopped. When I turned around, I saw a man duck into the entrance of a building.

This time the city looked different. Instead of the romantic City of Lights I'd seen on my way to Cuba, Paris now seemed brutal, congested, as alienating as New York, a city where tourists could enjoy the sights and never think about peasants who lived in hovels on the other side of the world. The people who lived in the five- and six-story apartment buildings which lined the streets had once watched as their fellow citizens were sent off to death camps—or even worse, many Parisians had collaborated in sending them off. Frenchmen with dirty hands and bloody hands, in respect to Southeast Asians and Algerians. The artists and poets who were romanticized in the books written for tourists had often starved in these streets.

Then, as these thoughts went through my head, I realized they were the kinds of things Christina or Felicia might have said.

It was the middle of summer, but Paris seemed dismal and cold to me. Yet it was the same city as on my first visit. The narrow, winding streets which had charmed me then annoyed me now as I tried to find the police station. What had I found so beautiful? Even the language sounded like a tape recorder on high speed, and no doubt it was presently communicating the same sorts of inanities which consumed the lives of Americans. Rushing through the streets, ignoring each other, the people seemed rude and self-centered. Unlike the Cubans, they weren't going to invite you into their homes for coffee or to share a meal.

My French didn't go far with the cop I talked to. But he spoke enough English to think I was possibly dangerous. After a brief conversation, he stepped into another room. Fearing he might be calling the American Embassy, or that he might arrest me, I hurriedly left.

Back at the hotel I looked for Monica. She'd left a note in the room saying she was following BJ. From Bloomberg I learned that BJ and Sharon were going to the Louvre, so I headed there. At least Paris had a good transportation system. I got to the museum in less than twenty minutes. But I was tired. All night I'd been trying to sort things out—Christina's relationships with Fuentes and Adolfo, Art Sparrow's refusal to listen to my warning, the peace movement, civil rights, and BJ's involvement with radicals. As I searched the maze of galleries, my mind wandering, I suddenly felt exhausted. In spite of my fears for Sharon—and Monica—I had to go into one of the museum coffee shops to sit and rest for a minute.

I ordered a coffee. Then, before I could drink it, I dozed off. I couldn't have been asleep for more than a few minutes. I dreamed about San Francisco Bay, about being stranded in the middle of an ocean. And then I was driving through suburbs. It was twilight. I was heading for a house in East Los Angeles. As I turned a corner, I hit an animal. It appeared so suddenly that I must've hit it mid-air. I stopped, got out of the car, and saw an enormous deer with giant antlers lying in the middle of the road. What was it doing here? I had to do something. I ran to a door and rang the doorbell. There was a window in the top of the door. Through the thick, distorting glass I could see people in the dining room of the Havana Riviera. I knocked harder. A man got up and came towards me. It was Jake Campbell.

"I've hit an animal," I said. He shook his head but wouldn't open the door, so I ran across a lawn to the next house. But I could see the animal struggling to its feet.

"There's a hurt animal," I said. It was Sharon who answered the door. "I was turning the corner. The last rays of the sun were coming through the trees, blinding me."

"I watched the sunset myself," she said. No, it wasn't Sharon. It was Felicia. "The dying sun was deep red, like blood."

"We've got to get help."

"Is it still alive?"

As she looked past me, I heard a terrible sound—the animal's breath. It had gotten to its feet. Its back was crooked, white bone protruding from its side, blood pouring from the wound. It collapsed, and I ran to it.

"Put it out of its misery," Steve Bloomberg said. Dick Thornton, Frank Vara, and the others members of the group were coming out of different houses.

"Are you going to do something?" This was Christina, in a swimming suit, standing next to Maria Montalvo. "It's cold here. We can't stand around forever."

"I have no gun," I said.

"Use a knife then," Christina said.

The animal stared up at me. A shudder ran through its body. It was trying to get up but didn't have the strength. I ran to my car for a tire iron. When I came back, the group had gathered around—Art Sparrow, Monica, Helen Anderson.

"I was turning the corner," I said. "It was an accident. I had no idea animals like this live around here."

Jake Campbell, wearing a dinner jacket, stepped forward. "What are you going to do with that?" he said, pointing to the tire iron.

Christina stepped out of the crowd. "Would you like something to drink?" she said.

"What about this animal?"

"Don't worry about him."

It was dark. I felt cold. The animal was obscured except for the top of his head and face and his antlers, which reflected the streetlights.

"It must have come down from the mountains," someone said. "It's still alive."

"But it's dying," I said. A strip of light fell across its head. The eyes continued to stare at me.

There was a scream as I raised the tire iron. For a second I paused, and in that second the creature somehow got to its feet. Then I delivered a crushing blow to the back of its skull.

The crowd turned away. The animal and I were alone on the deserted street. I sat down, exhausted, and lay my head on its still-warm body.

"He was magnificent," somebody said behind me.

"You should have seen him leaping through the air," I said. "And what antlers!"

When I opened my eyes, it took me a few seconds to remember where I was. At first I thought I was back in Carlsbad, Czechoslovakia, because Jan Hutoc, the man Christina Ward had introduced me to in a café there, was sitting on the other side of my table. But we were in a coffee shop at the Louvre in Paris.

"May I join you?" Hutoc said. And without waiting for a reply he added, "I understand Miss Ward had an accident in Cuba."

I was still too surprised by Hutoc's appearance to speak.

Hutoc lit a cigarette, sucked in smoke, then held the cigarette upright between his thumb and forefinger. "In Carlovivari we discussed Castro versus Tito. Do you remember? Of course you do. I told you that many of us Czechs applauded Tito for standing up to the Russians."

Was I still dreaming?

Hutoc continued. "Oh, yes. It was a great thing, you know. I asked you and Miss Ward if you thought the Cubans would have the strength to do that, to stand up to the Russians. You said you would tell me after your trip. So then, what do you think? Do they have the courage?"

"What are you doing here?" I finally said.

"Miss Ward said she would write to me. She was going to send me pictures. I'm quite curious about Cuba, you see. I am wondering now, do you know of these pictures?"

"Christina's things were sent back to the States."

"To whom, I wonder. I don't believe she had family there." He extended his lower lip and sucked on his cigarette again. "But didn't she give you something to deliver to me?"

I shook my head.

"What about her camera? She didn't give you her camera? As a keepsake or a gift? Because there was no camera in her things, as you refer to them."

"She did have a camera, but it was sent to the States."

"I'm so disappointed, Mr. Aucielo. I was looking forward to pictures from Cuba." Hutoc stood. "Well, it's been a pleasure. Perhaps we will see each other again." He dropped his cigarette in his coffee cup and cocked his head slightly to look at me one last time. Then he turned and left.

I decided to ask Jake Campbell for help. From Monica I learned that Campbell and Bloomberg were meeting in Campbell's room with someone who had arrived from the States. Monica believed they were planning tactics for our arrival at the New York airport. They expected customs officials to confiscate our passports and the FBI to arrest us.

"Jake wants newspapers and TV to be there," Monica said.

I went to Campbell's room and knocked. Bloomberg answered the door. Inside, I could see Lou Corbett, a member of the People's Revolutionary Party who must have flown in from New York. I said I needed to talk to Campbell.

"We're in a meeting," Bloomberg said.

"This is truly a matter of life and death."

The door closed. A minute later Campbell came out to the hall.

"I hope this isn't about the wild tale you've been trying to peddle around here," he said. "My advice is that you ought to shut up before you find yourself arrested or locked up in an insane asylum."

"While Johnson is free to kill."

"If I find out you're responsible for the Cubans shoving us on a plane so fast, I'll break your neck myself." Campbell started to go back inside, then hesitated. "Are you pissed because as an anti-Communist you can't stand the idea of BJ joining our party?"

I caught up with Johnson at the hotel in the early evening as he and Sharon were heading to dinner. Monica was sitting by the window, pretending to read. As they left, she came up to me.

"I've been waiting for you."

I asked her to come with me. As we followed Sharon and BJ, I again went over my suspicions.

"That's still not much evidence," Monica said. "And BJ really doesn't look the type."

"Did Art Sparrow look like a government agent? What's a murderer supposed to look like?"

We followed BJ and Sharon along the Rue de la Roquette to Bastille, then down Boulevard Henry IV to the Seine, and then across the river to a restaurant in the Latin Quarter. It was a half-hour walk, but not once, although I was sure BJ was aware of us, did he turn around.

While they ate, we watched the restaurant from across the street. After a long meal, they came out and walked leisurely through the Latin Quarter. They finally stopped at a bar on Rue Saint Jacques. This time Monica and I followed them inside. We sat near the door. They were at a table at the far end of the bar. Besides Sharon and Monica, the only female in the place was the bartender. The customers—all of them Arab men—drank strong mint tea and occasionally got up to dance by themselves to the recorded music. Hashish was openly being passed from table to table. I declined. BJ did not. Neither did Sharon. While I was watching them, an old man was dancing—I couldn't decide whether he had the face of a child or of Methuselah, maybe both alternately. Monica said, "That guy, the one with the knife, was at our hotel today."

"What guy? What knife?"

"The guy who just came in. He's cutting a piece of fruit at his table."

BJ divided his attention between the dancer, Sharon, and us. When Sharon finished her tea, they both got up and walked out without looking at us. We waited a minute, then followed. BJ was standing outside, waiting for me. He greeted me with a punch to the face.

The blow knocked me against a wall. He followed the first punch with others. I thought I was going down, but I punched back as hard as I could. Johnson was big and athletic, but once I started fighting back,

I knew I was hurting him. Then, before either of us could do serious damage, somebody grabbed my arms, and somebody else inserted himself between me and Johnson. It wasn't anyone from the bar. It was Steve Bloomberg and Jake Campbell. Lou Corbett continued to pin my arms behind my back, and Sharon and BJ were allowed to walk off. They went in the direction of the Seine. When they disappeared, Corbett let go of me. I think the three of them were both ready to have a go at me, but some Arab men came outside and insisted we join them for tea. The comrades declined and walked off toward the river.

Monica and I agreed that Sharon was safe, at least for the present.

The next day was sunny. With my camera I waited in the hotel lobby for BJ and Sharon to come downstairs. Then I followed them to a café, then onto the subway, and then through the narrow, winding streets of Monmartre. The whole time I was following them, I was aware that Steve Bloomberg was following me. And behind Bloomberg was the man who had been cutting a piece of fruit at the Arab bar the night before.

BJ and Sharon ate lunch in a square near the Sacre Coeur Cathedral. Then Sharon bought some trinkets, and the two of them looked out over the city. I was sore, bruised, and tired. Occasionally BJ would turn and stare at me. Sharon would tug his arm, and he'd smile at her and ignore me for awhile. Bloomberg stayed close by. The guy behind Bloomberg stayed farther away as we walked back down the hill, through Clichy, and all the way to the Champs-Elysees and the Arc de Triomphe. Here, BJ and Sharon disappeared into a metro station. I wasn't too worried. I'd made my accusations, and so many people knew that BJ and Sharon were together that I thought she was safe.

32

In the morning we made the final leg of our journey, Paris to New York. At the airport, the People's Revolutionary Party—Jake Campbell, Steve Bloomberg, Sharon Albright, Helen Anderson, and Lou Corbett—surrounded BJ. On the airplane, whenever I got up, one or two of them would get up also. If BJ had hired a private guard, he couldn't have had better protection.

This was our fourth flight across the Atlantic. When I went through my suspicions with Monica again, they seemed more convincing to me than ever. Four rows ahead of us, joking and laughing, sat a handsome, charming killer.

Monica said, "I did see him sneaking around the hallways of the Hotel Riviera, but I figured that like everyone else he was going to somebody's room to get laid. You know, I was jealous." Monica also said that that morning Campbell had told her that I was a gusano.

"Anyone who doesn't agree with Jake is a gusano," I said, "or a counter-revolutionary Trotskyite."

"I guess I don't rate any more," she said. "Jake says I'm just a petit bourgeois intellectual. What are you going to do when we get to New York?"

I said I'd get the police to take a close look at Johnson.

I couldn't sleep because I kept seeing BJ at Felicia's door on Precita Avenue. When she answered, he smiled at her, and, knowing him, she invited him inside. When her back was turned, he attacked.

"The photos," I said to Monica. "You heard him in the lobby. Didn't he say something about me taking pictures of Felicia?"

"He said something about shocking photographs."

"But how would he know about those pictures—unless he'd taken them?"

"He said he heard about them from the police."

I tried, but was too tired to remember what the police had said about photographs.

We were greeted in New York by flashbulbs and a flurry of questions from a crowd of reporters. I was a bit surprised that our defiance of the travel ban was still news. Immigration officials wanted to confiscate our passports, but, as directed by Jake Campbell, the group refused to hand them over, and wouldn't proceed through customs until Immigration backed down.

Jacob Campbell, in all his glory, made a speech to the television and the press. The main attraction, however—and the big surprise—was when William "BJ" Johnson fell to his knees, kissed the ground, and shouted how wonderful it was to be back in the Free World. All the photographers except me got shots of him smiling and handing over his passport and going through customs accompanied by two men in suits. A swarm of reporters, eager to hear the condemnations he was making against communism and Cuba, followed him and his escorts. Sharon, Jake, and their comrades watched this display of patriotism with shocked expressions. And I could do nothing, not even take photographs of the circus, because four policemen immediately placed me under arrest— for the murder of Felicia Vasquez. BJ left the airport surrounded by reporters and flanked by the two men in suits whom I now recognized as Art Sparrow and Dr. Marcus.

I was allowed to telephone my boss, Mrs. Wilson, and ask her to get me a lawyer and get me out. I also told her my suspicions about BJ. A few hours later I was visited by a civil liberties lawyer who promised I'd be out of jail within hours. I told him about BJ Johnson. The lawyer said he'd talk to the police for me.

But it was six days before I got out. For most of this time I was alone with my thoughts. On the outside, Americans were watching *Mary Poppins* and *My Fair Lady*, and a man named William "BJ" Johnson was on the loose. Where was he? What was he doing? Who was he stalking? Were the police paying any attention to my pleas?

During this time I had plenty of time to think about my fellow travelers. Probably they were now doing what they'd been doing in

Cuba—arguing, complaining, making speeches to their friends, screwing, eating and drinking, spying and gossiping.

Dr. Marcus and FBI Agent Paul Larson visited me on the third day.

"We want to talk you about your trip," Larson said.

"Let's talk about Bill Johnson," I said.

"You met Che Guevara, and you had meetings with Captain Lima, a man close to Guevara. What did you meet with Lima about?"

"We talked about the murders of Christina Ward and Maria Montalvo. Johnson killed them. He's the one who killed Felicia Vasquez and maybe Anne Montrose and maybe others we don't know about."

"We've heard this accusation," Larson said.

"You're not taking it seriously though. Why is that?"

"About Johnson?"

"He's working for you, isn't he?" I said. "That's why you're protecting him. You had his arrival all planned, didn't you? That's why there was so much news coverage. I'll bet he was working for you in college too. You guys escorted him out of the airport. Where'd you take him?"

Neither Marcus nor Larson responded. Finally Larson said, "The Cubans have made some bizarre allegations. Are these what you cooked up with Lima?"

"You're looking for political conspiracies and plots—as I was—and your minds are so occupied with the Cold War that you won't or can't think of anything else. Do you know where BJ is now?"

Neither man responded.

"I'd like to talk to Art Sparrow."

Larson shook his head.

I did learn one thing from Marcus and Larson. No charges had been filed against Clifton Specks, and he'd been released soon after arriving back in the States.

It wasn't until Detective Stringfield talked to me by phone from San Francisco that I knew I'd begun to get through to the cops. My lawyer had talked to Stringfield and learned that although there had once been a warrant for my arrest, issued by the San Francisco police, it had been cancelled. The New York police finally confirmed this. The Berkeley police, however, wanted to talk to me, but only about the men who had set fire to the offices of the Fair Play for Cuba Committee.

"I thought gusanos had killed Felicia," I told Stringfield. "Then I thought the People's Revolutionary Party was behind it. In Cuba a woman named Christina Ward was killed in virtually the same manner as Felicia, and then a Cuban woman named Maria Montalvo. Anne Montrose, who drove with BJ, me, and three others from San Francisco to New York, seems to be missing and may be one of his victims. Also, a balcony railing at my hotel in Cuba was tampered with so that I almost fell eighteen stories. I'm sure Johnson was behind all these things."

Stringfield told me that he and Detective Mantz had questioned Johnson as part of their investigation into Felicia's murder, but there had been no reason to hold him. And, of course, by the time I talked to Stringfield, BJ had disappeared.

"We're watching his mother's house," the detective said. "She lives in the Sunset district. That's where he grew up."

"The Sunset," I said. BJ Johnson was not the son of rich socialites. He had come from the same neighborhood I had.

"The last anybody's heard," my lawyer said, "Johnson set off driving across the country with somebody who put up an advertisement in Greenwich Village to share driving and expenses from New York to California. But nobody knows where he is now."

Not since Felicia's death, not since I'd left San Francisco, not on the drive across the country, not in Europe, not on the tour of Cuba, perhaps not in my life up to now, had I ever thought so carefully. Perhaps if I'd been thinking carefully before, I might have saved lives. I remembered BJ speaking at Felicia's memorial. I remembered him speaking to the Mothers of Cuban Martyrs. I remembered him on Cuban television. Perhaps if I'd been more attentive…

This was also when I began remembering things about the neighborhood where both of us had grown up. I tried to imagine what this person felt when he killed. I thought about Felicia, and of course about Cuba and the People's Revolutionary Party. What was wrong with socialists and communists? At the top, there always seemed to be the Jake Campbells, ready to take advantage. Were people like Johnson just products of capitalist society, or of all societies—past, present, and future? And I wondered if Cuba, as Che believed, could break this pattern. In jail I wrote my last article for the series Mary Wilson had called "Travels with Che and Fidel." I ended it by quoting Guevara, who had said that socialism can only be nurtured in an atmosphere of freedom—not merely freedom from hunger, but freedom from all coercion which distorts the soul of man. I wrote that the Cuban Revolution would ultimately be judged by this moral standard. I also tried to analyze his ideas about the transformation of man from a self-centered creature to an altruistic being. At one moment these ideas seemed profound. Then, when I thought about BJ Johnson, they seemed utterly utopian.

At my first meeting with Guevara, after the group interview, he'd promised to help in the investigation of Christina's death. At our second meeting, the night before we left Cuba and the night I gave Captain Lima the photos Christina had hidden amongst my own, Che had apologized for his inability to conclude that investigation satisfactorily.

33

Besides the inconvenience of spending almost a week behind bars, the main effect of my arrest was that Johnson disappeared into the North American continent. Also the value of my Cuba photos depreciated.

I learned from Anne Montrose's sister that Anne had still not returned to Berkeley. Although she was not an officially missing person, no one knew where she was.

When I finally got back to San Francisco, the first thing I did was talk to the police. They had only my word about the conversation in Paris, the conversation in which BJ had alluded to the pornographic photos of Felicia. Both Detective Stringfield and Detective Mantz said they hadn't mentioned any photos to Johnson. And neither of them was aware of any pornographic pictures. Monica, who was back in San Francisco, confirmed my story about BJ's taunting me about pornographic photographs.

A serious investigation of BJ Johnson was already underway. Detectives Mantz and Stringfield had gotten a search warrant for Johnson's apartment in Berkeley, but the apartment had been thoroughly cleaned and refurnished by the new tenant. They'd also visited Johnson's parents and checked with the Berkeley police about unsolved murders of young women. Oakland, just south of Berkeley, Richmond to the north, and Martinez to the east, all had their share of unsolved murders or disappearances of young woman going back three and four years. But there was nothing to link these cases to Johnson.

I tried on my own to find out where he was. Sharon Albright had come to the Bay Area to work for the Student Committee to Uphold the Right to Travel, and she had addresses and phone numbers for everyone who'd been on the trip. She gave me the numbers she had for Johnson when we met for coffee at the Mediterranean Café on Telegraph Avenue.

After apologizing and thanking me for saving her life, which now I didn't really think had been in danger, she said, "It's so hard to believe. We all lived with him for weeks. I thought I knew him. And he'd done good things."

"Good things?"

"He was part of the Montgomery bus boycott. He worked with Martin Luther King, Jr. And he worked with a clinic in South America—"

I didn't think any of this was true. And as for idea that she had been in danger of possibly becoming one of Johnson's victims, I'd concluded that although he'd shown interest in her, she wasn't really his type. But I didn't argue. I listened, hoping Sharon might be able to shed some light on Johnson's personality.

"At the end of the trip, everyone thought we were a couple," she said. "But we were just friends. I mean—you know what I mean. I enjoyed it for a while. Every girl in our group, and practically every girl in Cuba, was flirting with him. Then I thought maybe he was homosexual, one of those men who just likes women for friends, or who dates or even gets married so people won't know. Anyway, we never, you know, went to bed together. When you said those things, when you accused him, I thought you were insane. But when he kissed the ground at the airport, I was really shocked. He'd been lying to everyone. He was a cop all the time. What I don't understand is how he could be a cop and some kind of madman killer. Did you know it was BJ, along with Jake of course, who asked me to lie about Christina being drunk in the swimming pool? Him and Jake. And I went along."

I asked Sharon what kinds of things BJ had talked about.

"Gossip," she said. "He gossiped a lot. He was nice to people, but he despised certain ones, like you, Dante. He hated you. I did too for a while. He said, 'The lady doth protest too much.' That was because of your questions about Felicia Vasquez. His parents—you know they died when he was very young. Sort of like the Rosenbergs, I think."

I didn't contradict Sharon, but instead thanked her for the address and phone numbers she gave me—although I was sure they were already out of date.

As anyone who's traveled knows, when you come home everything looks different. Cuba was my first extensive trip away from the Bay Area. When I walked with Camillo, the dog I'd inherited from Felicia, I saw, at least for a while, a strange city. I'd been away less than two months, but it seemed as if skyscrapers had shot up along the skyline, and my grandfather's friends had suddenly moved to the suburbs, leaving him and a few other old-timers behind.

In one of my old pictures, a photo of a group of Civil Rights activists, I found BJ Johnson standing with a group of students. But he looked different because he'd been wearing a mustache. I compared this photo with the ones I'd taken in Cuba, and showed them to Detectives Stringfield and Mantz. My point was that Johnson could easily change his appearance.

My favorite photo of Felicia was a picture of her standing on a cliff at Big Sur. I'd enlarged this photo and given it to her, and she'd put it on a wall in her bedroom. Now I tried to remember seeing it in her apartment the day I'd found her. I was positive it hadn't been there. Unfortunately I no longer had the negative. Hoping to get a copy, I wrote to Mirta Vasquez and asked if she had that picture, and if she did, to make me a copy. Mirta wrote back, promising to send me a copy.

Through a contact who worked at the University I got the addresses and phone numbers of Johnson's parents, who, contrary to what Sharon Albright believed, were very much alive. No doubt the police already had this information, but they weren't sharing it. I first went to visit Johnson's father, William Johnson, Sr., who was living in Seattle and worked as an accountant. We sat on his porch where his second wife served us coffee, and Johnson told me he'd been separated from BJ's mother for many years. His children by his first marriage, BJ and Lindsey, had blamed him for the divorce. The last he'd heard of Lindsey, she was part of a group calling itself the "Diggers" and was living in Northern California. The last he'd seen of his son had been when BJ was elected student body president. I asked if there had been any problems with the law when BJ was growing up. Johnson seemed to be thinking about this as he looked into the distance. It was a beautiful day. To my surprise, he began crying.

"I don't know what happened," Mr. Johnson said. "What did I do wrong? Sometimes he would lie, sometimes steal. He could look right at you and tell the most outrageous nonsense. If he had a choice between a lie and the truth, he'd tell you the lie, even if it didn't mean anything."

I told Mr. Johnson some of the things BJ had told Sharon. Johnson shook his head.

"To my knowledge he's never been to South America and was never part of the Mongomery bus boycott. That stuff came up when he ran for student body president, but I think he got away with those stories. But lies eventually catch up with a person. This stuff about the girl—is it true? Maybe he got in with the wrong crowd, hippies maybe, and he's taking the rap. Because I don't think he could do anything like that."

Next I located the commune where Johnson's sister, Lindsey, had lived—she was now in India—and I met her former boyfriend, Alex, a guy with a beard and long hair.

"Her brother's a pervert," Alex said. "That's what Lindsey told me. She said he won the election for college president by stuffing ballot boxes."

Alex, however, didn't know exactly what the sister had meant by calling BJ a pervert. I told him about the women BJ had killed.

"There are at least three we know for sure about."

Alex shook his head.

I got corroboration about Johnson stuffing ballot boxes in the student body elections from one of his former colleagues on the student body council. This woman said Johnson had been unscrupulous.

"He defaced the posters of his opponents and went around telling the most outrageous lies and violated every rule in the book," Darlene Holt said. "Nobody caught on until it was too late. You don't expect behavior like that in a campus election. By the time we had all the evidence against him and were about to take him to student court, the year was almost over. So he went out of office quietly. But you know what? He got accepted to graduate school. You know what department? Criminology."

The police were watching BJ's mother's house, and I didn't want to be accused of interfering with their investigation, so I saved Marjorie Johnson for last. It turned out to be a typical day in the Sunset, foggy and windy. I usually avoided the neighborhood where I'd grown up. The houses, new then—I'd played in them as they were being built—now had cracking plaster and were in need of paint, and some of the sidewalks, laid over the sand dunes, were buckling. These were the ticky-tacky houses Malvina Reynolds sang about.

Marjorie Johnson's house was only a few blocks from the house where my parents still lived. It was near McCoppin Square Park, on a street I must have passed hundreds of times. It might even have been one of the houses I'd looked into that night when I was eight years old and got lost coming home from the movies. I hadn't known BJ or his sister, but they'd gone to the same schools I had, played in the same parks, and had gone to the same theater. I rang Mrs. Johnson's bell, and waited. Then I rang again. Finally an old lady with bluish-white hair answered the door. I said I'd called earlier, and that I was her son's college friend. Mrs. Johnson invited me inside.

Mrs. Johnson had pictures of herself on almost every wall, and she immediately began showing me these pictures, as if I'd come expressly to see them. She described each photograph, when and where it had been taken. The pictures of her younger self struck me. She'd been a small, pretty woman with long, dark hair that fell over her shoulders and down her back. Her maiden name had been Rodriguez.

Mrs. Johnson paid close attention as I talked about BJ's "adventures" in Cuba. I didn't mention anything about the murders, although the police must have already been here and must have explained their investigation of her son. Answering me in confidential tones, Mrs. Johnson said that her son was on a secret mission for the government and was abroad somewhere. Occasionally he telephoned, but she never knew where he was calling from. He also sent home parcels for her to store. But she hadn't seen him for months.

I said, "I gave BJ my research paper to read. It was only a copy, but now I've lost the original. I was wondering if he left it here. I wouldn't ask, but if I could find his copy, it would save me a lot of trouble."

"Well, he has things in the basement," Mrs. Johnson said. "I have my housekeeper store his things down there for safe-keeping." She escorted me to the door which led to the basement. Fortunately she didn't want to follow me down the narrow staircase.

BJ's boxes were stacked in a room at the back of the basement. Most of the boxes were filled with books. Others were filled with clothes. There were some with dishes and silverware. There was a small television and a radio. On top were the most recent boxes, which contained pamphlets and books he'd sent home from Cuba. Looking for something that might incriminate him, I began digging through his things. After twenty minutes Mrs. Johnson called down to ask if everything was all right. I said I'd just be a few more minutes, and kept looking. But nothing seemed suspicious. Disappointed, I re-packed the boxes. When I finished, I took a quick look through the rest of the basement. There were several pieces of furniture stacked atop each other, bicycles, a box of empty bottles, more boxes of books, a workbench with tools, and on one side a washing machine and a dryer. Mrs. Johnson called down to say she'd made tea and was waiting for me. Just to be sure I hadn't missed anything, I went back to the workbench where I'd seen a flashlight, and shined a light under the stairway. A piece of canvas had been thrown over more stuff. I lifted the canvas and found more junk—a lamp, a chair, a box of ceramic knick-knacks, and an old chest, which was locked. I went back to the workbench, got a hammer, and snapped the hasp on the chest. It was filled with old magazines. I started to close it. Then it occurred to me that it was strange to store magazines in a locked chest. On top were *Look* and *Life* magazines, but beneath those I found an assortment of pornographic and martial arts magazines. But these magazines still proved nothing, and I went back upstairs.

Mrs. Johnson's housekeeper, Mrs. Daniels, had arrived for the day. She'd thrown out the tea Mrs. Johnson had made and had brewed a fresh pot. The middle-aged black woman stood by the stove while I drank tea. She said Mrs. Johnson had gone into the living room to rest.

"It's her nap time. I come in two hours a day. I do the shopping and fix her meals."

I asked Mrs. Daniels what she knew about Johnson, his travels and his "work for the government." She shook her head. I decided to take a chance, and told her what I was really looking for, and I explained why. The woman studied my face as I spoke. Finally she said, "You and the police and the Army won't find anything in a million years, just like they couldn't find them boys in Mississippi. The reason is you don't know where to look." She stood up. "Why didn't they tell me about them girls? Come on now. Follow me."

I followed Mrs. Daniels upstairs to a bedroom which was still reserved for Johnson. The room was immaculate. I watched as the housekeeper went over to a closet and got down on her knees. It took her a few minutes. Then she brought out a small metal box and handed it to me.

"I know where everything is," she said, out of breath. "I don't know what's inside, but I know it's secret. He buries it way back in a little place."

I telephoned Detective Stringfield and told him what I'd found in Johnson's bedroom. Stringfield got a proper search warrant, and then he, Detective Mantz and I returned to Mrs. Johnson's house.

"You can see in some of these pictures that her neck was already broken," Stringfield said.

It was difficult for me to look at Felicia lying naked and dying. I brought Stringfield into the hallway to look at the photographs of Mrs. Johnson which covered the walls. He shrugged.

34

Later I had another errand in the Sunset. A visit to my parents, to whom the FBI had been sending my articles, annotated with comments about my pro-Communist reporting. Most of my family—aunts, uncles, cousins, but not my grandfather, who had already heard about the trip—were there to hear about my adventure. My mother had prepared sandwiches with the crusts cut off, aunts had brought salads and cakes, and when I arrived everyone was eating. I got a cup of coffee and took it into the living room. Then, while my relatives sat and listened and watched me, I explained the corruption and poverty which had ruled the island before Castro, and talked about the housing, schools, and hospitals built since the Revolution. Finally, as in my *Free Express* articles, I voiced my criticisms, especially the lack of democracy.

As I spoke, the room grew quieter and somehow threatening. After hearing about Communist atrocities for decades, these good and patriotic Americans could not believe there was anything valuable in the Caribbean experiment. They stared at me. They exchanged glances and whispered to each other. By the time I mentioned BJ Johnson, who had lived only a few blocks away and was still on the loose—and who had been protected by the FBI—the aunts, uncles, and cousins had begun to leave. I was about to leave, myself. My brother stopped me to let me know that I'd surely hurt his career, and my father said that he didn't understand how I could become a Communist and throw my life away. Walking to my car, I remembered again how, when I was eight years old and had been lost, I'd gone up to several houses to look through the front windows. The houses were virtually identical to each other. As a child I had turned the windows into picture frames to allay my terror. It was a neat and comforting trick of the mind, turning reality into a photograph.

At the request of the San Francisco police, I wrote Captain Lima in Cuba to ask about the status of the investigations into the deaths of Christina Ward and Maria Montalvo. I heard nothing from Cuba until the end of November, when Lima wrote to tell me that unfortunately he had nothing new to report on either of the deaths. He added that a Cuban delegation would be in New York in December, and that I would receive an invitation from the Cuban Mission to the United Nations to attend a reception. When Mrs. Wilson learned that Che Guevara would be speaking at the United Nations, she bought me an airline ticket to New York. I was glad not to have to drive again across the continent.

The reception took place on the night after Guevara's speech to the General Assembly. It was held at the Cuban Mission, which was heavily guarded and filled with dignitaries. When it was my turn to be introduced to the minister, Guevara shook my hand and gave me an envelope containing a medal typically given to vanguard workers in Cuba. I'd already collected several of these vanguard worker medals from the factories and farms I'd visited, and it wasn't until I was back in San Francisco that I looked at the back of the medal and found an inscription. "Truth is a powerful weapon of the Revolution." The card in the envelope said, "Thank you for your articles. Che Guevara."

In the story I wrote for the *Free Express*, I quoted from Che's U.N. speech and also from the Second Declaration of Havana. A month later I got a subpoena to appear before the House Un-American Activities Committee.

At the time of the hearing, President Johnson was talking about The Great Society and escalating the Vietnam War. Steve Bloomberg, Sharon Albright, and Helen Anderson, along with a few dozen of their comrades and friends, faced a phalanx of police who were guarding the committee room. Jacob Campbell had been called to appear, along with Richard Thornton, me, and a surprise witness. Campbell came in dressed as an American colonial soldier. The first person to be called, he tried to disrupt the hearing, and was found in contempt. Thornton testified about "the propaganda the student group had been fed by the Cubans," and about the plans of the People's Revolutionary Party to subvert the United States government. Then, to my surprise, my old friend and roommate, Charley Jessup, who hadn't even been on the Cuba trip, was called. Charley said that he'd declined to go on the trip when he'd learned its real purpose was to further communism. He then read a statement which echoed the testimony of Richard Thornton. While he was on the stand, Charley didn't once look at me. But, after all, his testimony didn't amount to much.

I had prepared a statement which I read to the Committee. Afterwards I published it in the *Free Express*. It read in part:

"I toured Cuba during July, 1964, with a group of other Americans, mostly students. The members of this group did not hold any particular beliefs in common except the belief in their right to travel and to see Cuba for themselves. I was a journalist, sent by the *Berkeley Free Express*, to cover this trip, which was organized by the Committee to Uphold the Right to Travel and paid for by the Cuban Federation of University Students. I was invited because the organizers of the trip felt my reporting was fair and that the coverage they would get in other media would not be. I was under no pressures from either the Committee or from the Cubans to do anything but report what I saw. Along with the other members of the group, I met Fidel Castro, Raul Castro, Ernesto Guevara, Oswaldo Dorticos and other Cuban officials, as well as a delegation from the National Liberation Front of Vietnam. I am not a member of any political party, nor am I an agent of the Cuban government. My observations about Cuba have already been published."

Against the Committee's objections, I then added that there had been two deaths on the trip which were not accidents but were committed by one of the members of our group, William "BJ" Johnson, who on his return to this country had kissed the ground and praised the United States. I said that Johnson had probably been employed and protected by United States government agencies, and that he was still at large.

But where was he? BJ had disappeared.

35

Che Guevara also disappeared. He left Cuba in 1965 and was reported to be in Algeria in February, and in the Congo the following year. But his disappearance really dates from March, 1965. His farewell letter and resignation of all offices and Cuban citizenship are dated October of that year. We know now that Che returned to Cuba from the Congo, and then, disguised and carrying a forged passport, left for Bolivia.

After the Gulf of Tonkin Incident in 1965, the Vietnam antiwar movement grew rapidly. The pictures I had been shown by the Vietnamese in Havana—pictures of peasants carrying weapons through the jungle, pictures of villages bombed, pictures of houses and people burning—became commonplace in the American media. I, along with tens of thousands of others, became an antiwar activist. Although I was the main reporter for the *Free Express* on Latin American affairs, I was also covering the war and the antiwar movement.

By 1967, BJ Johnson had been missing for three years. He was still very much a concern of mine, and I continued to correspond with Mirta Vasquez about any leads in the case, although none of them brought the police any closer to capturing Johnson.

In October of 1967, the world learned of Che's death. The night I heard about it I was covering a rally on the Berkeley campus of the University of California. Thousands of students had gathered in Sproul Plaza to prepare a protest march on the Army Induction Center in Oakland. One of the speakers was Monica Chapman, whom I still saw frequently. She read the message Che had sent to the Tricontental Conference.

"Create two, three, many Vietnams," Monica said into a microphone. "Of what difference are the dangers to a human being or a people, or the sacrifices they make, when what is at stake is the destiny of humanity?"

Che's resurrection on posters and T-shirts, in films and musicals, had not yet happened. Pictures of him were not yet decorating college dormitories. But his words found their mark. The crowd cheered. When Monica said that Che's severed hands would haunt his enemies, I thought of the movie I'd seen with Sharon Albright in Havana, *The Beast with Five Fingers*. And I thought that we create our own beasts. As students lined up at the speakers' platform to denounce the war, I was reminded of a book Felicia Vasquez had loaned me. The book described how young Trotsky escaped across Siberia in a troika to join the revolution in Europe. I was also reminded of the young people I'd met in Cuba, like our guides, Ricardo Martinez and Maria Montalvo. Now these young Americans were being summoned to their own troikas, to cross their own Siberias.

Monica ended her speech by quoting Che again. "Wherever death may surprise us," she said, "let it be welcome if our battle cry has reached even one receptive ear, if another hand reaches out to take up our arms, and others come forward…"

The next day, when the students marched to the Army Induction Center in Oakland, their numbers had grown to such a degree that for blocks the streets around the Induction Center were jammed. The police declared the demonstration an illegal gathering and shot tear gas into the crowd. Chaos broke out. Chased from one street, protestors ran to another. Cars were pushed away from curbs, fences were torn down, and debris was piled up at intersections to make barricades. I covered the event and took pictures. Monica was there, bullhorn in hand, attempting to control the crowd.

People surged toward the Induction Center when the buses carrying draftees finally came into view. I worked my way through the crowd, hoping to get pictures of the young men and their responses to the protest. The closer I got to the buses, the more chaotic and violent the pushing and shouting became. I was about to give up when I saw a familiar figure. At first I could see only his back, but then, as he turned, I recognized the smiling face. It was BJ Johnson, decked out in army fatigues, directing a squad of military police and pointing to his right. Several MPs headed in that direction. Then Johnson turned and looked out at the crowd. Perhaps he was calculating the strength of the enemy. Standing at the top of the steps of the Induction Center and flanked by military police, he could have been a poster model for a clean-cut, handsome, all-American soldier. No wonder the police hadn't found him. He'd disappeared into the army, and was an officer no less. He shouted something to his troops. I was just one face among thousands, but, as if he could feel my gaze on him, he turned and looked directly at me. Our eyes met—at least I think so. The next minute he was gone, guiding the draftees through the doors of the Induction Center.

It seemed like ages before I could work my way back through the crowd and find a telephone. I tried calling Detective Stringfield in San Francisco. Then I tried Mantz. Finally a Detective Sykes came on the line, and I tried to explain that I'd just seen William Johnson, who was wanted by the San Francisco police and by the FBI for murder. Sykes said he'd call me back.

Stringfield didn't get my message until later that day.

"If he's in the army," Stringfield said, "we'll get him."

The army claimed there was no William Johnson, officer or not, who had been on duty at the Oakland Induction Center the day of the "riots." And of course there were hundreds of William Johnsons serving in the armed forces. The process of identifying BJ's photograph took days. Finally police photos were matched with a decorated soldier who had served two tours of duty in Vietnam, and had come to Oakland only a week earlier. His name, according to the United States Army, was Dante Aucielo, and while he had been given a student deferment, he had nevertheless enlisted in September of 1964. Among other things, the Aucielo-Johnson file contained photostats of my birth certificate and my high school and college diplomas. How had BJ gotten my records? Then I remembered the night I'd found Camillo locked in the bathroom of my apartment and Felicia's photos spread out on the floor. At the time I'd assumed I'd been drunk. Of course, I couldn't know for certain that BJ had sneaked into my apartment then and had stolen these papers. He might have done it later. In any case, by the time his true identity was established by the army, he'd gone AWOL and disappeared again.

36

For a while, I kept track of the people I accompanied to Cuba. Jacob Campbell, I know, did well in the sixties and seventies when his organization recruited dozens of college students, along with their trust funds. The last I heard, his printing company was doing jobs for the New York Stock Exchange. Monica Chapman became a professor of Women's Studies. Some years after our trip I ran into Steve Bloomberg, who was trading in pork bellies on the stock exchange, and who'd grown a sizeable belly himself. Sharon Albright became an activist in the Peace and Freedom Party. Helen Anderson became a lawyer. Richard Thornton was a member of the Black Panther Party and had spent some time in jail before ultimately starting a church in East Oakland. Frank Vara remained in Cuba. Arlene Washington became a social worker in New York City. I saw my old roommate, Charley Jessup, twice after the HUAC hearing. The first time he confirmed what I'd guessed—the FBI had given him the choice of testifying against me or facing drug charges. The last time I saw him, he was pushing a cart full of aluminum cans and had lost most of his teeth.

In America, if you refuse to check your brains at the door, if Socrates—not Jesus or Horatio Alger—is your role model, you will probably find yourself alone. Friends I had before the Cuba trip, and most of my family, broke relations with me, I believe, because my articles, unlike the rest of the American media, did not portray Castro and Guevara as monsters, and because I wrote about the suffering forced upon the Third World by the United States. It's blasphemy to suggest that American privileges might be related to that suffering.

Art Sparrow was right. In the mid-seventies, when the *Free Express* went out of business, I was unable to get a job with another newspaper. I sold articles freelance but wound up driving a cab for a few years, zig-zagging back and forth through the city all night, driving in circles. I felt

I was among the lost, and that no one could see a reasonable way out of the hell we'd created. So I drove the streets, stopping occasionally to take a photo or to write in my notebook, as if the act of documenting the old people I saw in all-night cafeterias, or the veterans sleeping in doorways, or the children playing in rundown tenements might lead, if not to paradise, at least to purgatory. I'd race my cab up Taylor Street to the hotels, then down the Mason Street hill and over to Fisherman's Wharf, then to the nightclubs on Broadway or the bars in the financial district. Up Market Street, back down Market Street, across the Bay Bridge, up Kearny to Broadway, out to the airport, restaurant to bar, bar to restaurant, hustlers on Polk, whores in the Tenderloin, drunks everywhere, loops and circles, circles and loops—these streets were, for a few years, my life.

Sometimes I'd pretend the windshield of my cab was a movie screen, and the music on the radio a movie sound track. Sometimes I'd park my cab at the top of the Hyde Street hill, where I'd look out at the bay.

Lights come on along the shores of the bay as fishing boats and freighters pass under the bridge. Clouds drift in from the ocean, and the sky darkens over the city. I watch the last rays of the sun behind Mt. Tamalpais. Sometimes I see, in the blackness over the water, a boy waiting to be rescued. Sometimes I see a tiny boat swamped by a gale. Night falls.

When I read about dissidents being imprisoned in Cuba, I wonder if Felicia's faith would have endured.

I dream about walking along the cliffs at Big Sur and photographing her as she looks out over the ocean. I remember the first time I saw her in a lecture hall, and later, when I saw her again and she laughed at me. I remember how, showing me pictures she'd taken in Cuba, she fell asleep on her couch in the apartment on Precita Avenue, how I was afraid to move because I didn't want to awaken her. I remember that when she opened her eyes that night, she smiled. Sometimes I dream that we're walking through a forest. She looks up at the roots of trees clinging to cliffs, and she says, so softly, "Sometimes trees grow in strange places."

In the dream I am happy, but there are tears in my lover's eyes, and I do not know why.

37

I am looking through the photographs I took in Cuba: Che, flanked by his aides, Captain Fuentes smoking a cigarette, Captain Lima apparently dozing in the July heat; Che, his arms propped on the conference table, his fingertips touching, his eyebrows raised. He looks intently at my camera, as if to communicate his ideas with absolute clarity. In another photo his hand is raised. My notes say he is discussing mistakes made concerning industrialization. Of course, the Soviets had already sabotaged Che's plans for industrialization. Nor would they tolerate his campaign against material incentives. In another photo he's frowning as he talks about the life of workers in the mines and latifundia of Latin America. And I wonder what he had seen as a young man that tourists never see, what he had seen that had made him climb onto his own troika, in his case a motorcycle. Of course, when I took these photos I had no idea this face would someday appear next to portraits of Jesus in peasant homes throughout Latin America and on posters and all over the world.

I've collected pictures taken by other photographers—Che holding children, playing baseball, swimming, talking to world leaders; Che in Bolivia disguised as Ramon Benitez Hernandez, with bald head and horn-rimmed glasses. Looking at this photo, I wonder if it's perhaps a view of the Guevara who might have been if he had chosen not to become a revolutionary.

When he was wounded and captured, Che is reported to have said, "Don't shoot! I'm Che Guevara, and I'm worth more to you alive than dead." We're not certain he said these words any more than we know if Jesus said, 'My God, my God, why hast thou forsaken me?' The next day Che was executed. Knowing he was about to be shot, he told the soldier aiming the machine gun to wait. And then he stood to meet death.

From the beginning of his Bolivian adventure, the odds were against him. Fidel, balancing Cuba's need for an extension of the Revolution with its dependence on the Soviet Union, was forced to make his support for Che secret. And there was Che's asthma, and there were the debilitating sicknesses which he and his comrades endured, and the hostile environment. Above all, there were betrayals, the Judases like Anibal Escalante, an old-line Cuban Communist, and Mario Monje, head of the Bolivian Communist Party—and even, perhaps, Christina Ward.

One last photograph: Che dead at age thirty-nine. This is the photo published around the world after his execution in the village of La Higuera, Bolivia, on October 9, 1967, before his hands were severed and his body hidden in an unmarked grave. His eyes are open, as if with sorrow and compassion. As Che was being executed, the President of the United States was anouncing his readiness to negotiate an end to the war in Vietnam. The next day Lyndon Johnson ordered the bombing of Haiphong Harbor.

When I visited Cuba in 1964, campesinos would gather in the Plaza of the Revolution and look up at the lighted windows in Guevara's office. It was said that the Commandante never slept. There was a joke current then. A counter-revolution has been successful, and the Cuban leaders are placed in a dungeon, each entombed in different amounts of shit according to the degree of their revolutionary zeal. President Dorticos has shit up to his knees, and Fidel stands in shit up to his chin, but the shit surrounding Raul Castro reaches only up to the waist. Fidel asks his brother why he has shit only to his waist, and Raul says, "Because I'm standing on Che's shoulders."

We didn't know it when we interviewed him in 1964, but even then Che was losing power. There was no place for him in the state he had helped to create.

Before my journey to Cuba, I had not in my wildest dreams imagined I would ever meet this man, let alone ask him to help me catch a murderer. As I look back on that journey, I wonder at my own blindness. I also wonder if Che's own blind spots were not similar to my own. I wonder if, indeed, it is these blind spots which continually frustrate our efforts to achieve justice. I was digging blindly, like those treasure hunters Felicia and I saw digging up a beach, but I was digging through stories and lies, real plots and imaginary plots, and finally I was digging through the photographs I'd taken…

I met Che Guevara three times. The first time was at the group interview in Havana in 1964 when I asked him about the cover-up of Christina Ward's death; afterwards he had called me into his office. The second time was in the lobby of the Havana Riviera when I gave to Guevara's assistant, Captain Lima, the photos of an old man. The third time was at a reception in New York City. But there may have been a fourth meeting. In 1966, although I was still obsessed with finding BJ Johnson, I was offered another trip to Latin America, this time to write articles exclusively for the *Free Express*. On a flight from Brazil to Bolivia, I had an aisle seat next to an elderly businessman who was coughing badly and had to get up frequently to use the toilet. Whenever I stood to let him pass, he would nod. He was bald except for a fringe of hair on the sides and back, and wore horn-rimmed glasses. I didn't pay much attention to him. There was no other interaction between us.

When we landed, I carried my camera pack through the aisle and down the stairway to the tarmac. At the bottom of the stairway, as I stopped to put my pack over my shoulder, the businessman who had been sitting next to me walked past. I suddenly remembered the photograph of the old man which had turned up amongst my other photographs in Cuba. When I looked again, the businessman was gone, vanished, absorbed by the crowd of businessmen, journalists, and common people entering the airport building.

Perhaps this was just another trick of the mind, like the 'photographs' I imagined when I was a lost kid on the way home from the movies. Or perhaps my eye was beginning to catch up with my camera. But for a moment I felt I was suddenly escaping the misery I'd been witnessing all over the continent… as if a troika were lifting and carrying me over these tragic mountains and rivers, forests and plains.

BOOKS BY ROBERT DAVIS
PUBLISHED BY LOST BOOKS PRESS:

IZ (1995)
Among the Lost (2009)
IZ Too (Available March 2010)

To order please send $12.00,
plus $2.00 for shiping and handling to:

Lost Books Press
PO Box 31438
San Francisco, CA 94131-0438

Or you may order online at
www.LostBooksPress.com